Love in Hopewell Creek

VIVIAN BELLE

STERLING RIDGE PRESS LLC

Dedication

For those who stand at life's unexpected crossroads, only to discover
they've arrived precisely where God intended them to be.
And for every heart brave enough to believe that somewhere, someone
is already preparing to receive the love they bring.
For in our most desperate moments of decision, we often find ourselves walking directly into our destined path.

Vivian

About The Author

Vivian Belle is a talented author known for her sweeping **Historical Christian Romance** novels set against the untamed beauty of the American frontier. With a deep love for history and storytelling, she brings to life **resilient heroines, steadfast heroes, and faith-filled journeys** in the vast, rugged landscapes of the past.

Nestled in the **majestic mountains of northern West Virginia,** Vivian finds endless inspiration in the rolling hills, winding rivers, and boundless sky that mirror the spirit of her stories. When she's not writing, she enjoys **kayaking on tranquil waters, hiking through breathtaking mountain trails, and, of course, getting lost in a good book.**

Vivian's novels capture the heart of **faith, love, and perseverance**—where strong women and honorable men overcome life's trials to find hope, home, and happily-ever-after. Whether she's exploring the great outdoors or crafting her next frontier romance, Vivian's passion for adventure and storytelling shines through in every word she writes.

You can find out more about Vivian and her latest releases at www.vivianbelle.com or follow her on social media for updates and behind-the-scenes glimpses of her writing process. Stay connected—you won't want to miss the heartfelt stories of love and family she has in store!

Also by Vivian Belle

Where the Heart Finds Home
Faith on the Frontier
Love in Hopewell Creek

Contents

Chapter 1   1

Chapter 2   12

Chapter 3   17

Chapter 4   28

Chapter 5   36

Chapter 6   41

Chapter 7   51

Chapter 8   61

Chapter 9   77

Chapter 10   85

Chapter 11   97

Chapter 12   110

Chapter 13   122

Chapter 14   127

Chapter 15   138

Chapter 16   151

Chapter 17   160

Chapter 18   172

Chapter 19   179

Chapter 20   183

Chapter 21   195

Chapter 22   200

Chapter 23   208

Chapter 24   213

Chapter 25   223

Chapter 26   232

Leave A Review   238

Chapter 1

The crash of shattering glass jolted Beth Beaumont from her sewing. Her needle pricked her finger as she flinched, a bright bead of blood welling on her skin. She closed her eyes briefly, counted to five, and set aside the torn shirt she'd been mending.

"Your fault!" Her father's voice boomed from the parlor. "If you hadn't insisted on paying the butcher—"

"What would you have us do, starve?" Her mother's voice, once melodious, now carried the rasp of constant arguing. "While you throw away every cent on cards and dice—"

"I was winning! I had a system!"

Another crash followed—likely the small vase that had somehow survived their previous arguments. Beth pressed her handkerchief to her bleeding finger and rose from her chair by the kitchen window. The April morning had begun quietly enough, with her parents sleeping off last night's escapades, while she prepared a simple breakfast for herself and started on the mending pile.

But peace never lasted long in the Beaumont household these days.

Beth moved to the stove, where a pot of beans simmered—their dinner for the third night this week. She stirred the meager meal mechanically, her movements precise despite the chaos erupting in the next room. Four years ago, she wouldn't have recognized this house or the people who inhabited it. Four years ago, her parents had attended church every Sunday, her father had managed a respectable accounting position at the mercantile, and her mother had hosted ladies' aid society meetings in their well-kept parlor.

Now, empty bottles gathered dust in corners. Playing cards spilled from table drawers. And the family Bible that once occupied the center of their parlor table sat neglected on a high shelf, a layer of dust testifying to its abandonment.

"You silly woman!" Glass crunched under heavy footsteps. "That was my mother's!"

"Was it? I thought you'd pawned all her things months ago!"

Beth set down her spoon and moved toward the parlor doorway, already knowing she would regret the intervention.

Her father stood over her mother, his once-handsome face flushed with anger and drink, though it wasn't yet noon. At forty-five, Richard Beaumont looked a decade older, with bloodshot eyes and a trembling hand that no longer kept ledgers, but rather clutched betting slips and playing cards. Her mother, Caroline, sat on the worn settee, arms crossed defiantly, her blonde hair—the same honey shade as Beth's—hanging limp around a face too lined for its thirty-nine years.

Between them lay the shattered remains of her grandmother's crystal candy dish.

"Please," Beth said quietly. "That's enough."

Her father whirled, noticing her presence. His face shifted, anger temporarily giving way to shame before hardening again. "Stay out of this, Elizabeth."

"I made beans for dinner," she said, ignoring his command. "They'll be ready soon."

Her mother laughed, a hollow sound. "Beans again. How fitting for the grand Beaumont family. Tell me, Richard, is this what you promised when you swept me off my feet? Beans while you gamble away our lives?"

"If you'd just let me finish the game last night—"

"Then what? We'd be living in a mansion? Like the one you lost three years ago with your 'sure thing'?"

Beth stepped between them, physically inserting herself into the argument. At twenty, she was tall enough to look her father in the eye, though his broad frame still dwarfed her slender one.

"Father, please. Mother. Remember who you are—who we once were." Her voice softened. "Remember when we used to pray together before meals? When you taught Sunday school, Mother?"

Both parents fell silent, the mention of their former lives striking some remnant chord of memory. For a moment, Beth saw a flicker of recognition in her father's eyes—a glimpse of the man who had once carried her on his shoulders after church and taught her to add columns of figures at his desk.

But the moment passed. Her father pushed past her, grabbing his coat from the hook by the door.

"I don't need reminders of the past from my own daughter," he muttered. "I'm going out."

"Richard!" Her mother rose, suddenly alarmed. "We have nothing left! The rent is due."

"Then pray for a miracle, Caroline," he sneered, throwing her words back at her. "Isn't that what you used to tell everyone at your precious church gatherings? God provides?"

The door slammed behind him, rattling the few remaining intact picture frames on the wall. One tilted, then fell, the glass fracturing across a faded family portrait taken when Beth was sixteen—before the first bad investment, before her father's dismissal from the mercantile, before the drinking and the gambling took hold.

Her mother stared at the broken frame, then at Beth, something vacant behind her eyes. "Clean that up, would you? I have a headache." She turned toward her bedroom, pausing only to add, "And don't hold dinner for me. Or your father."

Beth knelt beside the broken frame, carefully extracting the photograph from the shards. Four smiling faces looked back at her—her parents, herself, and her brother William, gone four years now, buried in a soldier's grave near the Mississippi. His death had accelerated her parents' decline, grief transforming into a bitterness that found solace in vice.

She traced her finger over William's face. "I don't know what to do anymore, Will," she whispered.

After gathering the glass fragments, Beth returned to the kitchen and checked the beans, adjusting the heat beneath the pot. She moved to the window, looking out at the street beyond. Once, their home had sat in a respectable St. Louis neighborhood. Now, the area had declined along with their fortunes, housing those whose dreams had slipped from their grasp.

A newspaper lay on the kitchen table, delivered early that morning. Beth hadn't had time to read it yet, her morning consumed with chores. She sat down, needing a moment's respite from the weight of her household duties.

The front page bore news of railroad expansions westward and territorial disputes. Beth flipped through the pages mechanically, barely registering the words, until her eyes caught a small advertisement in the classifieds section:

GODLY MAN SEEKS BRIDE

A Christian gentleman of sound character and means in Hopewell Creek, Colorado Territory, seeks a God-fearing woman of good disposition for marriage. Must be willing to relocate to a growing frontier town with a strong church community. Comfortable home and respectable position await the right woman. Contact Henry Dobbins, General Delivery, Hopewell Creek, Colorado Territory.

Beth's fingers stilled on the paper. She read the advertisement again, then a third time. The words seemed to leap from the page——"Godly man," "church community," "comfortable home." Everything her life currently lacked.

Colorado Territory. So far from St. Louis, from the wreckage of her family, from the daily heartbreak of watching her parents' slow destruction.

A knock at the front door interrupted her thoughts. Beth hastily folded the newspaper and moved to answer it, smoothing her simple gray dress as she went.

Mr. Hilton, their landlord, stood on the porch, his ledger tucked under one arm. "Miss Beaumont," he said, removing his hat. His expression held a mixture of discomfort and determination.

"Mr. Hilton." Beth attempted a polite smile. "My father isn't home at present."

"Yes, well…" He cleared his throat. "That's becoming rather a pattern, isn't it? I've come about the rent. It's overdue—again. And I've been more than patient these past months."

Beth's heart sank. "I understand. Perhaps if you could come back tomorrow—"

"Miss Beaumont." His voice softened slightly. "I've heard those words from you before. Three months now with partial payments or excuses. I've respected your family—your father was once a well-regarded man in this community—but I have my own obligations."

"What are you saying?" Though she already knew.

"I'm saying you have until the end of the week to settle the account in full, or I'll have no choice but to begin eviction proceedings." He looked genuinely regretful. "I'm sorry."

The door closed behind him, and Beth leaned against it, her thoughts racing. Where would they go? What little money she managed to save from her seamstress work went to food and essentials. Her father's occasional employment never lasted—no businessman would keep a clerk who appeared with shaking hands and alcohol on his breath. And her mother had long since sold her jewelry and better dresses to support her husband's vice.

Beth returned to the kitchen, her gaze falling again on the newspaper. The advertisement seemed to call to her, promising escape, promising a return to the values that had once defined her family.

But could she truly leave? Abandon her parents to their self-destruction?

And if you stay? a small voice whispered inside her. Will you save them, or will they pull you down with them?

From her mother's bedroom came the muffled sound of sobbing—a common occurrence now, though one her mother would deny if confronted. From outside came the distant church bells marking noon.

Beth remembered when those bells had summoned them to worship, her family walking together in their Sunday best, her father leading with firm steps, her mother's gloved hand gentle in hers.

That family existed now only in memory.

Making a sudden decision, Beth moved to her small bedroom at the back of the house. From beneath her mattress, she withdrew a small cloth pouch containing her savings, carefully hidden from her father's increasingly desperate searches for funds to support his gambling.

She counted the coins and bills, calculating quickly. Enough for a train ticket to Colorado, perhaps. The thought sent a flutter of anxiety through her stomach. Marrying a stranger—was she truly considering this?

Yet, what were her alternatives? To watch her parents' continued decline? To be evicted and join the growing numbers of desperate women who populated certain St. Louis neighborhoods, selling themselves in ways Beth refused to contemplate?

Her gaze fell on the small wooden cross that hung on her wall—the last gift William had made for her before leaving to join the army, carved from a piece of oak with his pocketknife. It was simple, imperfect, but a reminder of faith and love.

"Lord," she whispered, closing her eyes. "I don't know if this is Your will or my desperation speaking. But I need guidance. Show me the path forward."

No lightning struck. No heavenly voices spoke. But as Beth opened her eyes, a strange calm settled over her. Perhaps this was her answer—not a miraculous intervention, but the quiet certainty that something had to change.

She pulled her trunk from beneath her bed and began to pack. Into a smaller bag, she tucked her savings.

Beth wrote a brief letter to her parents, explaining her decision without revealing her exact destination. She couldn't bear the thought of her father following her to Colorado, seeking funds for his next game. She left the letter on her neatly made bed, penning a separate note to Mr. Dobbins that she would post before boarding the train.

The house remained quiet as she worked, her mother's sobs having subsided into the deep sleep that often followed her emotional outbursts. Beth moved to her parents' bedroom door, opening it slightly to check on her mother.

Caroline Beaumont lay curled on the bed, an empty bottle on the nightstand beside her. Her face, even in sleep, held lines of discontent and sorrow. Beth remembered a different mother—one who sang hymns while baking, who read Bible stories aloud on Sunday afternoons, whose laugh brightened their home.

"I love you," Beth whispered to the sleeping form. "I always will. I pray you find your way back to yourself someday."

She closed the door gently and returned to her preparations. By mid-afternoon, her trunk was packed and her mind resolved. She would leave the following morning, taking the early train west.

***

Morning arrived with pale spring sunlight filtering through the window. Beth dressed carefully in her best walking dress, a simple navy-blue cotton with minimal trim. She arranged her honey-blonde hair neatly, secured her hat with pins, and donned her only pair of gloves, mended many times but still presentable.

She made one final circuit of the house, memorizing its details, before retrieving her small trunk and bag. At the door, she paused, listening for any sound from her parents' rooms, but heard nothing. Perhaps it was better this way—no tearful goodbyes, no recriminations, no false promises.

The walk to the train station took nearly an hour, her trunk growing heavier with each block. By the time she arrived, her arms ached and perspiration dampened her collar despite the cool morning air. The station bustled with activity—travelers coming and going, porters hauling luggage, vendors selling newspapers and refreshments.

Beth approached the ticket counter, her heart pounding. "One ticket to Denver, please," she said, her voice steadier than she felt. Denver was the closest major stop to Hopewell Creek, according to the station map she consulted.

"That'll be eighteen dollars and seventy-five cents, miss," the clerk said, barely glancing up.

Beth counted out the money, each coin and bill representing hours of careful work and painful sacrifice. When she handed over the fare, she felt a moment of dizzying panic. There was no turning back now.

The clerk passed her the ticket. "Track three. Boarding in twenty minutes. Denver's the third day out."

"Thank you." Beth clutched the ticket, her lifeline to a new future. Before boarding, she posted her letter to Henry Dobbins, informing him of her interest in his advertisement and her expected arrival date in Hopewell Creek.

The train stood waiting, belching steam into the morning air, its black iron form both intimidating and promising. Beth handed her trunk to a porter and found her seat in the third-class section—all she could afford. The wooden bench was hard, the space cramped, but it mattered little. Each turn of the wheels would carry her farther from

St. Louis, from failure and despair, toward a future she could only imagine.

As the train lurched into motion, Beth gazed out the window at the city receding behind her. Somewhere in those streets, in a declining neighborhood, her parents still slept, unaware that their daughter had chosen a different path. Would they miss her? Would they understand her decision? Or would they simply pawn whatever possessions she'd left behind for a few more hours at the gambling tables and drink?

Beth closed her eyes against the pain of these thoughts. "Lord," she prayed silently, "watch over them in their darkness. And guide me toward the light."

The rhythmic clacking of wheels on rails gradually lulled her anxiety. Beth felt something close to hope stirring within her. Hopewell Creek, Colorado Territory—even the name sounded promising. A creek of hope. A godly man. A church community.

A second chance.

She opened her eyes to watch the landscape changing outside her window. The city gave way to farmland, open fields stretching toward the horizon. Each mile marked a step into the unknown, yet Beth felt an unusual sense of peace. Whatever awaited her in Hopewell Creek, it offered the possibility of change, of renewal.

Beth reached into her bag and withdrew a simple envelope. Inside was the advertisement she'd cut from the newspaper. She traced the words with her finger—"Godly man," "comfortable home," "church community."

"Please be real," she whispered to the paper, to Henry Dobbins, to God Himself. "Please let this be Your plan for me."

The train whistle blew, long and low, as they approached a crossing. Beth tucked the advertisement away and straightened her shoulders. Three days to Denver, followed by whatever transportation she could arrange for the final leg to Hopewell Creek. A journey of nearly a thousand miles, each one distancing her from the shadows of St. Louis and drawing her toward an uncertain but hopeful future.

Beth gazed out at the passing landscape, watching America unfurl before her—vast and promising. Whatever lay ahead in Hopewell Creek, she was determined to face it with the quiet strength that had sustained her through her family's decline. This time, however, she would not be fighting to preserve what was lost, but building something new.

Something that, God willing, would last.

Chapter 2

Three days on the train left Beth sore, tired, and increasingly anxious about what awaited her in Colorado. The third-class accommodations offered little comfort—hard benches for sleeping, meager facilities for washing, and the constant noise and motion that made rest nearly impossible. Yet despite her physical discomfort, Beth's resolve remained firm.

The passing landscape had transfixed her—the vast plains giving way to rolling hills, then the distant, snow-capped peaks of the Rocky Mountains appearing on the horizon like sentinels guarding the territory beyond. So different from St. Louis, from anything she had known before.

As the train pulled into Denver's station on the afternoon of the third day, Beth gathered her few belongings, her legs unsteady after so many hours seated. The porter helped retrieve her trunk, and she stepped onto the platform, momentarily overwhelmed by the bustle and noise of the frontier city.

Denver was not St. Louis, but it carried its own energy—rawer, more immediate. Men in dusty work clothes mingled with merchants in suits. Women in practical frontier dress walked alongside those in Eastern fashions. The air carried the scent of livestock, coal smoke, and something wild and untamed that Beth couldn't quite identify.

She made her way to the station agent, clutching the newspaper advertisement. "Excuse me, sir. I need to reach Hopewell Creek. Could you direct me?"

The agent glanced up from his ledger, assessing her with practiced efficiency. "Hopewell Creek? A small settlement about seventy miles southwest. Train to Colorado Springs, then you'll need to hire a wagon or coach for the remaining distance. The next train leaves tomorrow afternoon."

Beth's heart sank. Another day of travel and additional expense she hadn't fully anticipated. "Is there somewhere nearby I might stay tonight? Something... modest in price?"

The agent's expression softened slightly. "Whitman's Boarding House, three blocks east. Tell Mrs. Whitman that Morton sent you—she might give you the weekly rate even for a single night."

"Thank you." Beth smiled gratefully, then hesitated. "And may I ask...do you know anything of Hopewell Creek? Is it a... respectable town?"

"Growing place. It's got a church, school, mercantile, newspaper, and several other businesses. Had some mining nearby that's played out, but the town's settled into its own. Decent folks, mostly." He eyed her more carefully. "You got family there, miss?"

Beth straightened her shoulders. "I'm to be married," she said, the words strange on her tongue. "To Mr. Henry Dobbins."

"Don't know him personally, but Hopewell Creek's a small enough place. If he's established there, he's likely known to all." The agent returned to his ledger. "Mrs. Whitman can probably tell you more—she hears all the news from outlying settlements."

With directions to the boarding house, Beth hired a boy with a cart to transport her trunk. The walk revealed a city in transition—new brick buildings rising alongside rough wooden structures, the clash of frontier necessity with growing civilization.

Mrs. Whitman proved to be a broad-shouldered woman with sharp eyes and a no-nonsense manner that reminded Beth of her Sunday school teacher from years past. She inspected Beth thoroughly before nodding approval at Morton's recommendation.

"Single women traveling alone—it's not what I'd wish for my daughters," she said plainly. "But times are changing, and needs must. You'll have the small room at the back—clean sheets, basin for washing, meals at seven and noon and six, no exceptions. Two dollars for the night, meals included."

The room was indeed small but blessedly private and meticulously clean. Beth washed as best she could with the provided basin, changed into her second-best dress, and made her way to the dining room promptly at six.

Half a dozen other boarders sat at the long table—two commercial travelers discussing mining equipment, an elderly couple on their way to visit their son in a nearby settlement, and a young woman not much older than Beth who introduced herself as a schoolteacher headed to a position in Boulder.

"And what brings you to Colorado, Miss Beaumont?" Mrs. Whitman asked as she served a hearty stew.

Beth hesitated, suddenly self-conscious about her situation. "I'm traveling to Hopewell Creek. To be married."

Conversation paused momentarily. "Mail-order bride?" the schoolteacher asked with frank curiosity.

Beth nodded, her cheeks warming. "Yes. To Mr. Henry Dobbins."

Mrs. Whitman set down her serving spoon. "Dobbins, you say?"

Something in her tone made Beth's stomach tighten. "Yes. Do you know of him?"

The older woman exchanged glances with her husband, who sat at the head of the table. "I believe I heard the name recently," she said carefully. "From a guest passing through. When did you last correspond with this gentleman?"

"I..." Beth faltered. "I haven't exactly corresponded with him yet. I answered his advertisement just before leaving St. Louis." She didn't mention that she'd only sent the letter three days ago, meaning it would arrive in Hopewell Creek long after she did.

Mrs. Whitman's expression grew concerned. "Miss Beaumont, might I have a word with you after dinner? In private?"

The remainder of the meal passed in polite conversation that Beth barely heard, her mind racing with possibilities. What had Mrs. Whitman heard? Was Hopewell Creek not the respectable community the advertisement had portrayed? Was Henry Dobbins known for some impropriety?

When the other boarders had retired to their rooms or the small parlor, Mrs. Whitman beckoned Beth to the kitchen.

"I don't wish to alarm you unnecessarily," she began, wiping her hands on her apron. "But I feel I should share what I know. A woman passed through here last month and mentioned this Dobbins fellow. She, too, said she was on her way to marry this man. My dear... you need to be cautious."

Beth felt a chill pass through her body despite the warmth of the kitchen. "Another woman? Are you certain it was the same, Mr. Dobbins?"

Mrs. Whitman nodded gravely. "No, I cannot be sure it is the same man you speak of. He could have a brother, I supposed. This woman had letters with her—several of them—and spoke quite confidently of her impending nuptials."

Beth sank onto a kitchen chair, her legs suddenly unable to support her. Doubt crept into her mind. The advertisement had been purposefully vague, promising much while revealing little about the man himself.

"My dear," Mrs. Whitman said gently, "I've seen many young women pass through these doors over the years. Some fleeing something, some chasing dreams. I don't know your circumstances, but I urge caution." She placed a weathered hand over Beth's. "At least send a telegram ahead to confirm arrangements before proceeding further."

Beth stared at their joined hands, her mind whirling. A telegram would cost precious money from her dwindling funds. What if the other woman had been mistaken, or lying? What if Mrs. Whitman was not remembering correctly?

"I will," she said finally. "Thank you for your kindness in warning me."

That night, Beth slept fitfully, her dreams filled with faceless men making promises they never intended to keep.

Chapter 3

Beth's body lurched forward as the train to Colorado Springs jolted into motion, the sudden movement nearly toppling her from the hard wooden bench. She grabbed the edge of her seat, steadying herself as the locomotive's whistle pierced the morning air with a long, mournful wail.

The Denver station receded through the smudged window, taking with it Mrs. Whitman's warnings. Each turn of the iron wheels carried her deeper into uncertainty, closer to Hopewell Creek—and to Henry Dobbins, a man whose face she couldn't picture.

"First time out this way, miss?"

Beth turned to find an elderly woman settling beside her, arranging her plain brown skirts with practiced efficiency. Her face bore the weathered lines of someone who had spent decades under the western sun, but her eyes sparkled with warmth.

"Yes," Beth admitted.

The woman nodded knowingly. "You'll find the territory's got its own way about it. Land's harder, people too, sometimes—but there's a kind of freedom in it." She extended a work-worn hand. "Martha Holloway. Returning to my son's ranch outside of Colorado Springs."

"Beth Beaumont." She shook the offered hand, grateful for the simple human connection. "I'm traveling to Hopewell Creek."

"Hopewell Creek?" Martha's eyebrows lifted. "That's a fair piece beyond the Springs. Family there?"

Beth hesitated, heat rising to her cheeks. "Not yet. I'm... to be married."

Understanding dawned in Martha's eyes. "Mail-order bride, then?" When Beth nodded, the woman patted her hand. "Nothing to be ashamed of, dear. Half the women west of the Mississippi came that way, myself included, thirty years ago. Who's the lucky fellow?"

"His name is Henry Dobbins." Beth reached into her reticule, withdrawing the folded newspaper advertisement. "He placed this notice."

Martha squinted at the paper, then handed it back without comment, though something flickered briefly across her face—concern, perhaps, or doubt. Beth's stomach tightened. Had this woman, too, heard something about Henry Dobbins?

"Do you know him?" Beth asked, unable to keep the worry from her voice.

Martha shook her head. "Can't say that I do. Been a few years since I visited Hopewell Creek." She studied Beth's face. "You haven't met him, then? Or seen his likeness?"

"No. It was... rather sudden, my decision to come."

The train lurched around a bend, the rhythmic clacking of wheels on tracks punctuating the conversation. Outside, Denver's outskirts gave way to open country, the landscape rolling toward distant mountains.

Martha's expression softened. "Well, I won't pry into your reasons, dear. But let me offer some advice if I may. When you arrive in Hopewell Creek, before you meet this man, find the minister. Pastor Paul, if he's still there. A good man, fair-minded. Tell him your situation. In these small towns, the preacher knows everyone's business, the good, and the bad."

Beth swallowed hard, an uncomfortable knot forming in her throat. "You think I should be cautious?"

"I think," Martha said carefully, "that a young woman alone in an unfamiliar place should always have her wits about her, especially when her future's at stake." She reached into a woven basket at her feet and withdrew a cloth-wrapped package. "I packed enough food for an army. Would you care to share?"

The simple offer of food—homemade bread, cheese, and sliced apples—eased the tension. As they ate, Martha spoke of her son's ranch, her grandchildren, and the changes she'd witnessed in the territory over three decades. Beth listened gratefully, allowing the woman's steady chatter to soothe her frayed nerves.

When Martha dozed off an hour later, Beth turned her attention to the window. The landscape had begun to change dramatically, the flat plains yielding to gentle foothills. In the distance, the Rocky Mountains rose against the sky, their peaks crowned with snow despite the spring warmth below. The sight stole her breath—so vast, so unlike the crowded streets of St. Louis.

From her small traveling bag, Beth withdrew her Bible, its leather cover worn soft with years of handling. It had been her mother's gift on her sixteenth birthday, before the gambling and drinking had consumed their home. She ran her fingers over the embossed cover, then opened to a familiar passage in Isaiah that she'd marked with a pressed flower.

"Behold, I will do a new thing; now it shall spring forth; shall ye not know it? I will even make a way in the wilderness, and rivers in the desert."

A way in the wilderness. Beth glanced at the rugged landscape outside. Wasn't that precisely what she sought? A new path, a fresh start, away from the wilderness her life had become in St. Louis?

Her gaze fell again to the newspaper advertisement. "Godly man," "church community," "comfortable home." The words that had drawn her halfway across the country. She tried to imagine the man behind them—honorable, faithful, kind. A man unlike her father had become.

But Mrs. Whitman's warning nagged at her. Another woman, also traveling to marry Henry Dobbins? It could be a coincidence, a misunderstanding. Or it could mean she was traveling toward another disappointment, another betrayal.

The train whistle sounded again, jolting Beth from her thoughts. As if sensing her disquiet, Martha stirred beside her.

"Wool-gathering?" the older woman asked, straightening her bonnet.

"Just thinking about what lies ahead." Beth managed a smile. "And praying for guidance."

Martha nodded approvingly. "Faith's a good companion on any journey." She peered out the window at the changing landscape. "Especially in this country. Out here, you'll find yourself closer to God's handiwork than perhaps anywhere else. The mountains have a way of making a person feel small and significant all at once."

"I've never seen mountains before," Beth admitted, her gaze drawn again to the distant peaks. "They're... overwhelming."

"That they are. Beautiful and dangerous together, like most worthwhile things in life." Martha studied Beth's profile. "May I ask, dear—what brought you to answer an advertisement from a man you've never met, in a place you've never seen?"

The question, though gently posed, struck at the heart of Beth's vulnerability. She hesitated, uncertain how much to reveal to this stranger, kind as she seemed.

"My circumstances in St. Louis became... untenable," she finally said, choosing her words carefully. "My family..." She faltered, unwilling to speak ill of her parents despite everything.

Martha waited patiently, her weathered face free of judgment.

"My family changed," Beth continued. "After my brother died in the war, my parents... lost their way. Lost their faith." The admission felt both painful and liberating. "There was nothing left for me there."

"And so you seek a fresh start," Martha concluded. "There's no shame in that."

"But is it wrong?" Beth asked, voicing the doubt that had haunted her since leaving. "To abandon them?"

Martha considered this. "The Good Book tells us to honor our father and mother. That's true. But it also tells us there's a time to plant and a time to pluck up that which is planted. A time to break down, and a time to build up." She patted Beth's hand. "Sometimes honoring your parents means not watching them destroy themselves—and not letting them destroy you in the process."

The words struck Beth with unexpected force. She had never considered her departure in those terms—as an act of preservation rather than abandonment. Tears pricked at her eyes, but she blinked them away.

"Thank you," she whispered.

"Now," Martha said, her tone lightening, "tell me about your skills. What does a young woman from St. Louis bring to frontier life?"

The conversation shifted to practicalities, and Beth found herself sharing her abilities—cooking, sewing, basic household management, the bookkeeping she'd learned from her father in better days. Martha offered advice on what might prove useful in a place like Hopewell Creek, from preserving food to managing a kitchen garden.

"The town's grown since I was last there," Martha said. "Used to be just a mining camp, really, but from what my son tells me, it's established itself proper now. The mine played out, but the town survived."

"What can you tell me about it?" Beth asked eagerly.

"Well, it's situated pretty, near a creek that gives it its name. Surrounded by good grazing land, so there are cattle ranches nearby. The church was just being built when I visited—a simple place, but the community was proud of it. There's a general store, a smithy, a saloon, or two." Martha frowned slightly. "Can't recall hearing about a man named Dobbins, though."

The train began to slow, approaching a water stop. Passengers stirred, some rising to stretch their legs during the brief halt. Beyond the window, a small cluster of buildings marked a settlement barely worthy of being called a town.

"I think I'll step out for some air," Beth said, needing a moment to gather her thoughts.

Outside, the spring sunshine warmed her face, a welcome change from the stuffy train car. Other passengers milled about the platform, smoking, chatting, or simply enjoying the brief respite. A group of men huddled near the water tower, their conversation carrying in the clear air.

"—another mining outfit buying up claims in Hopewell territory," one said, puffing on a pipe. "Offering good money too, from what I hear."

"Won't amount too much," another replied. "Those hills been picked clean years ago."

"Tell that to the Eastern investors throwing money at it," the first man laughed. "More dollars than sense, those fellows."

Beth moved away, their conversation holding little interest for her. At the edge of the platform, she gazed toward the mountains, now seeming closer, more imposing. A single hawk circled lazily in the blue sky, riding thermal currents with effortless grace.

The scene transported her suddenly to a Sunday afternoon from her childhood—her family picnicking by the river, her father pointing out a similar bird soaring above. "See how it trusts the wind?" he'd said. "That's faith, Beth. Knowing you're held up by something you can't see."

The memory came with such clarity that Beth could almost feel the grass beneath her, hear her mother's laugh, see William skipping stones across the water's surface. Before the war. Before the gambling. Before everything fell apart.

"Miss? You all right?"

Beth turned to find a young boy watching her curiously. She realized her cheeks were wet with tears she hadn't felt falling.

"Yes," she said, quickly wiping them away. "Just thinking of home."

"You going far?" he asked, with a child's directness.

"Hopewell Creek."

"My pa went there once. Said it was a good town, 'cept for the man who cheated him at cards." The boy shrugged. "Pa says there's a cheat in every town, though."

Before Beth could respond, a woman called sharply, and the boy ran off. The train whistle blew, summoning passengers back aboard. Beth took one last look at the mountains before returning to her seat.

Martha had laid out more food—a piece of cold chicken, a biscuit, and a small jar of preserves. "Eat," she instructed. "The dining car's prices would rob you blind, and you'll need your strength."

They ate as the train resumed its journey; the landscape growing more dramatic with each mile. Low hills gave way to steeper terrain, and the track began to wind through cuts and around curves. The clatter of wheels took on a different rhythm, almost musical in its complexity.

"Near halfway to Colorado Springs now," Martha remarked, gathering the remains of their meal. "We should arrive by early evening."

"And from there to Hopewell Creek..." Beth said.

"That's the harder part for you. You'll need to catch the stage, but they don't run daily. Might be a wait."

Beth nodded, calculating her dwindling funds. Each delay meant another night's lodging, another meal in a strange place. She had been frugal, but her resources were limited.

As if reading her thoughts, Martha said, "If there's no stage right off, my son would put you up for a night. His ranch is a fair distance from town, but he comes in regular for supplies."

"I couldn't impose," Beth protested.

"Nonsense. Josiah and Lydia have a proper guest room that sits empty most of the time. They'd welcome the company." Martha's eyes twinkled. "Besides, Lydia would appreciate another female presence. Being surrounded by menfolk wears on a woman sometimes."

Beth smiled gratefully. "Thank you. I'll remember your offer if needed."

The afternoon wore on, the train steadily climbing higher into the foothills. The car grew more crowded at each stop, filled with miners, farmers, families, and the occasional well-dressed businessman. The air thickened with tobacco smoke, the scent of unwashed bodies, and the indefinable smell of human aspiration and desperation mingled together.

Across the aisle, a young family caught Beth's attention—a tired-looking woman with an infant and a toddler squirming on her lap. The husband stared stoically ahead, his calloused hands resting on knees patched so many times the original fabric was barely visible.

The woman caught Beth's gaze and offered a weary smile. The gesture stirred something in Beth—a recognition of shared womanliness, of vulnerability, of determination. Would she someday be that woman, traveling with children on her lap, a husband at her side? The thought both frightened and enticed her.

Her attention shifted as a commotion erupted several seats ahead. A man's voice rose above the train's noise—slurred, belligerent.

"Told you to keep your filthy hands off my bag!"

Other passengers shifted uncomfortably. The conductor appeared, making his way down the aisle toward the disturbance.

"Sir, please lower your voice. You're disturbing the other passengers."

"Don't tell me what to do!" The man stood, revealing himself as tall, broad-shouldered, with unkempt dark hair and several days' growth of beard. His clothes marked him as a laborer, or perhaps a miner, and the flush on his face suggested he'd been drinking steadily. "This trash was trying to rob me!"

The accused—a thin, frightened-looking boy of perhaps fifteen—shook his head vehemently. "I was just moving it off the seat, mister! So I could sit down!"

The conductor positioned himself between them. "That's enough. Sir, either return to your seat or you'll be removed at the next stop."

For a tense moment, it seemed the drunk might resist. His eyes, bloodshot and unfocused, swept the car, briefly meeting Beth's before moving on. Something in that gaze—wild, angry, unpredictable—sent a chill through her.

Finally, with a muttered curse, the man dropped back into his seat, glaring at anyone who dared look his way. The conductor spoke quietly to the boy, who nodded and moved to a seat farther back in the car. Gradually, the tension dissipated, replaced by the usual sounds of travel.

"Lord have mercy," Martha murmured. "There's always one, isn't there?"

Beth nodded, but couldn't shake the uneasiness the man's gaze had sparked. It reminded her too much of her father in his darker moods, when the gambling losses mounted and the liquor fueled his temper.

"Best to avoid that sort," Martha continued. "The frontier draws all kinds—good people seeking opportunity, but also those running from something, or those whose vices have worn out their welcome elsewhere."

"And how does one tell the difference?" Beth asked quietly.

Martha considered. "Time reveals character, dear. But in the meantime, trust your instincts. The Lord gave us discernment for a reason."

Beth glanced again at the drunk, now slumped against the window, apparently asleep. Would her instincts serve her in Hopewell Creek? Would she recognize Henry Dobbins as a good man, or—her stomach clenched at the thought—would she discover too late that she had fled one bad situation only to land in another?

She withdrew her Bible again, seeking comfort in its familiar words. The Book of Proverbs had been her mother's favorite in better days. Beth turned to chapter three: "Trust in the Lord with all thine heart; and lean not unto thine own understanding. In all thy ways, acknowledge him, and he shall direct thy paths."

Direct thy paths. Beth traced the words with her finger. Was this journey truly God's direction, or merely her own desperate flight?

The question lingered as the afternoon waned. Outside, the shadows lengthened across increasingly rugged terrain. The train curved around a steep hillside, offering a breathtaking vista of the valley below. Several passengers, Beth included, gasped at the view—a patchwork of greens and browns, a winding silver river, and the mountains' blue haze beyond.

"God's country," someone murmured behind her.

Martha nodded in agreement. "Makes you remember how small we are, doesn't it? All our troubles and worries set against this vastness."

Beth could only nod, words inadequate to express the mixture of awe and insignificance she felt. St. Louis had its own majesty—the mighty Mississippi, the impressive buildings of commerce—but nothing that made her feel so directly confronted with creation's enormity.

As the sun descended toward the western peaks, the train began its final approach to Colorado Springs. Passengers gathered their belongings, children were roused from naps, and the general activity level in the car increased.

"Well, dear," Martha said, straightening her bonnet, "we'll soon be at the Springs. My son Josiah should be waiting—tall fellow, red beard, can't miss him. You'll come with us for tonight, and tomorrow we can inquire about the stage to Hopewell Creek."

Here's a rewritten version that enhances the exchange:

"You're very kind, but I must decline," she said softly. "Your company during the journey has meant more to me than I can express."

Martha's smile reached her eyes, warm with genuine sympathy. "Good luck, my dear," she whispered, gently squeezing her hand. "May God walk beside you every step of the way."

Chapter 4

The train whistled shrilly as it approached the Colorado Springs station, steam billowing past the windows. When it finally ground to a halt, passengers surged toward the exits, eager to stretch cramped limbs or greet waiting loved ones.

Beth gathered her small bag, following Martha through the press of bodies. On the platform, she was struck immediately by the quality of the air—crisp, thin, scented with pine. The elevation stole her breath momentarily, or perhaps it was the sight that greeted her: mountains rising almost directly from the edge of town, their massive presence unmistakable even in the gathering dusk.

The station platform bustled with activity—porters wheeling luggage, families reuniting with embraces, men in business attire striding purposefully toward waiting carriages. Beth stood amid the chaos, suddenly feeling very small and alone.

"There's Josiah," Martha exclaimed, waving to a tall man with a flaming red beard who towered above the crowd. "Are you certain you won't come with us, dear? It's no trouble."

Beth shook her head firmly. "I'm grateful, truly, but I should make inquiries about the stage to Hopewell Creek."

Martha's weathered face creased with concern. "At least let me introduce you to Josiah. He knows the stage schedules better than most."

Before Beth could protest, Martha had taken her arm and was guiding her through the crowd toward her son. Josiah Holloway proved to be as kind as his mother, his handshake firm but gentle, his eyes crinkling at the corners when he smiled.

"Miss Beaumont is traveling to Hopewell Creek," Martha explained. "When does the next stage leave?"

Josiah stroked his beard thoughtfully. "Not until tomorrow noon, I'm afraid. And it's a rugged journey—two days at least, with stops in three towns before Hopewell."

Beth's heart sank. Two more days of travel, plus tonight's lodging. Her remaining funds, carefully counted and recounted during the journey, would be stretched dangerously thin.

"Where will you stay tonight?" Martha asked, clearly reading the worry on Beth's face.

"I'll inquire about accommodations near the station," Beth said, trying to sound more confident than she felt. "Perhaps there's a respectable boarding house nearby."

Josiah exchanged a glance with his mother. "The closest boarding house is two streets over—Mrs. Colter's place. Clean enough, but she charges a dollar a night." He hesitated. "Mother's right, Miss Beaumont. Our home is open to you if needed."

"You're both very kind," Beth said, touched by their concern. "But I've imposed enough on Martha's generosity during our journey. I'll manage for tonight."

After further assurances, goodbyes, and Martha's insistence that Beth visit them should she ever return through Colorado Springs, Beth watched them go, an unexpected pang of loss tightening her chest.

Gathering her courage, she approached the ticket counter, where a harried-looking clerk was sorting papers.

"Excuse me, sir. I need to purchase passage to Hopewell Creek on tomorrow's stage."

The clerk barely glanced up. "Three dollars and twenty-five cents. Stage leaves at noon sharp."

The price was higher than she'd anticipated. Beth opened her reticule, counting out the money with fingers that trembled slightly. The transaction complete, she asked, "Could you direct me to Mrs. Colter's boarding house?"

"Two blocks east, then north, one block. White house with green shutters." He looked up properly for the first time, his expression softening slightly at the sight of her. "Though if you're looking to economize, miss, some folks just sleep here in the depot if they've an early departure. Station master allows it, long as you're quiet and don't make a mess."

Beth thanked him and moved away from the counter, weighing her options. Mrs. Colter's would consume a significant portion of her dwindling resources. The depot, while hardly comfortable, would cost nothing.

Outside the station, Colorado Springs revealed itself in the fading light—a mixture of frontier ruggedness and surprising sophistication. Gas lamps were being lit along the main street, their glow illuminating shop windows, restaurants, and the occasional saloon. The air held a bite of coolness despite the spring season, a reminder of the elevation.

Beth stood uncertainly on the station steps, her bag clutched in one hand, indecision keeping her rooted to the spot. The boarding house called to her with the promise of a proper bed, maybe even a hot meal. Yet, the money saved by staying in the depot might be needed later, in Hopewell Creek, if Henry Dobbins proved to be—

She couldn't complete the thought. Instead, she turned and reentered the station, finding a relatively clean bench in a corner away from the main flow of travelers. Setting her bag beside her, she settled onto the hard wooden seat, arranging her skirts modestly. At least here she was safe, surrounded by other travelers and station employees.

As the evening deepened, the station grew quieter. The last train of the day arrived and departed, leaving only those like Beth, who awaited morning transportation. A few commercial travelers dozed on benches, their luggage at their feet. An elderly couple huddled together, sharing a blanket against the growing chill. A young man in a soldier's uniform sat ramrod straight, staring at nothing, his face hauntingly reminiscent of William in his last photograph.

Beth shivered, drawing her shawl tighter around her shoulders. From her bag, she removed the remains of the food Martha had given her—half a biscuit and a small apple—and ate sparingly, knowing tomorrow would bring more travel with uncertain meal opportunities.

As the gas lamps were lowered for the night, leaving only minimal illumination, Beth settled back against the hard bench, trying to find a position that might allow some sleep. She thought of Martha in her son's comfortable home, of her parents in their St. Louis house that no longer felt like home, of Hopewell Creek and the unknown life awaiting her.

The sound of heavy boots on the wooden floor drew her attention. A man had entered the station—tall, broad-shouldered, with the slightly unsteady gait of someone who had been drinking. With a jolt of recognition, Beth realized it was the same man who had caused the disturbance on the train earlier.

He paused just inside the door, swaying slightly as his gaze swept the dimly lit room. When his eyes found Beth, a slow, unpleasant smile spread across his face. He changed direction, moving toward her with deliberate steps.

Beth's heart hammered against her ribs. She glanced desperately around the station—the attendant had disappeared into the back office. The other overnight travelers were dozing or lost in their own concerns. She was effectively alone with this approaching threat.

"Well, well," the man said, his voice carrying the same slurred edge it had on the train. "Ain't you a pretty little thing to find all alone."

He dropped heavily onto the bench beside her, too close, smelling of cheap whiskey and stale sweat. Beth clutched her bag to her chest, a pitiful barrier between them.

"Please leave me be, sir," she managed, her voice barely audible.

He leaned closer, his bloodshot eyes traveling over her face and down to her throat, where her pulse visibly raced. "Now, that ain't friendly. Just looking for a bit of company on a cold night." His hand moved toward her arm.

"The lady asked you to leave her be."

The voice, firm and clear, came from across the station. Beth looked up to see the young soldier rising from his bench, his posture straight, his gaze steady despite the shadows under his eyes.

The drunk turned, annoyance flickering across his face. "Mind your own business, boy."

"I'm making it my business." The soldier approached, stopping a few feet away. Though he was younger and less physically imposing than the drunk, something in his manner—a quiet authority, perhaps, or the hardness in his eyes—gave him presence. "Either walk away now, or I'll call the stationmaster and the local law."

For a tense moment, Beth feared the drunk would lash out. His hands clenched at his sides, his jaw worked as if chewing on his anger. Then, with a string of muttered curses, he pushed himself up from the bench.

"Ain't worth the trouble," he spat, swaying as he turned to leave. At the door, he paused to give Beth one last malevolent look before disappearing into the night.

The soldier remained standing until the man was gone, then approached Beth with a respectful distance between them. "Are you all right, ma'am?"

Beth nodded, unable to speak past the knot in her throat. Now that the threat had passed, she found herself trembling, reaction setting in.

"That fellow was on our train," the soldier said. "Caused trouble there, too." He hesitated, then gestured to the bench across from hers. "Would you mind if I sat? I promise I won't disturb you, but I'd feel better keeping watch in case he returns."

"Please," Beth managed, gesturing to the bench. "And... thank you."

He sat, arranging his uniform cap on the bench beside him. In the dim light, Beth could see that he was younger than she had first thought—perhaps twenty-two or twenty-three, not much older than her own twenty years. His face bore the look of someone who had seen more of life than his age would suggest.

"Wilburn Everett," he offered. "Recently discharged, heading to my sister's ranch near Pueblo."

"Beth Beaumont," she replied. "Traveling to Hopewell Creek."

"Family there?"

The question—the same Martha had asked—brought a flush to Beth's cheeks, visible even in the low light.

"No," she admitted. "I'm... to be married."

Understanding crossed his face, but unlike some who might have shown judgment or pity, he simply nodded. "My sister came out from Pennsylvania that way. She's happy now, three children and a good man who treats her well."

The simple statement offered more comfort than elaborate reassurances might have. Beth relaxed slightly, her trembling subsiding.

"My brother," she said softly, the words escaping before she could reconsider. "You reminded me of him just now."

Wilburn looked at her questioningly.

"He was a soldier too," Beth explained. "He died in '75."

Grief flashed briefly in the young man's eyes—the universal recognition of loss that connected survivors. "I'm sorry, ma'am."

"As am I for whatever you've seen." The bold statement surprised Beth herself, but something in Wilburn Everett's demeanor spoke of burdens carried too young.

He acknowledged this with a slight inclination of his head, neither confirming nor denying. From inside his uniform jacket, he withdrew a small flask. Catching Beth's startled look, he smiled faintly.

"Water," he said, offering it to her. "Not whiskey."

Beth accepted gratefully, taking a small sip of the cool liquid. "Thank you."

They lapsed into silence then, a companionable quiet between two strangers sharing a temporary haven. Beth relaxed against the hard bench, her body's need for rest overwhelming the discomfort of her surroundings.

"I'll keep watch," Wilburn said, correctly reading her exhaustion. "Rest if you can."

She should have protested, should have been concerned about propriety, but weariness won out. "God bless you, Mr. Everett," she murmured, allowing her eyes to close.

As sleep claimed her, Beth's last conscious thought was that perhaps divine guidance hadn't abandoned her after all. From Martha Holloway to Wilburn Everett, her journey had placed protective figures in her path just when needed most. Perhaps Hopewell Creek—and Henry Dobbins—would prove to be the sanctuary she sought, not another disappointment.

Chapter 5

The bench was just as hard when Beth awoke to gray dawn light filtering through the station windows. Her neck ached from its awkward position, and a chill had settled deep in her bones despite her shawl. Across from her, Wilburn Everett sat, his eyes alert, showing no signs of having slept.

"Morning, ma'am," he said quietly. "No trouble through the night."

Beth straightened, embarrassed to have slept while he maintained his vigil. "You should have rested, too."

A ghost of a smile touched his lips. "Habit from the service. Always someone on watch." He stood, stretching discreetly.

"Thank you for your kindness," Beth said, meaning it deeply. "I shall pray for your safe journey."

His expression softened. "And I for yours, Miss Beaumont."

With a respectful nod, James collected his modest belongings and moved toward the station door, pausing only to purchase a newspaper from the vendor just setting up his stand for the day. Beth watched him go, another fleeting connection in her journey toward an uncertain future.

The station gradually came to life around her. The elderly couple awoke, sharing a modest breakfast from their basket. Commercial travelers gathered their sample cases, heading out to conduct their business in town. The ticket counter opened, and a fresh-faced clerk took his position.

Beth used a small portion of her remaining money to purchase a cup of hot coffee and a simple roll from the station vendor. The food revived her spirits somewhat, though anxiety about the journey ahead still gnawed at her.

By mid-morning, the station had filled with travelers awaiting the noon stage. Beth secured a spot near the departure area, her trunk at her feet, watching as luggage was loaded onto the roof of the sturdy Concord stagecoach that would carry her to Hopewell Creek.

"Miss Beaumont?"

Beth turned to find a middle-aged woman in a practical traveling suit addressing her. Though they hadn't been introduced, the woman spoke with the confidence of an established acquaintance.

"Yes?" Beth replied, puzzled.

"Martha Holloway described you to me this morning at church." The woman extended a gloved hand. "Penelope Smith. My husband and I are traveling to Winsome Valley, which is on the Hopewell Creek stage route."

Beth shook her hand, still confused by the unexpected introduction.

"Martha was concerned about you traveling alone," Eleanor explained. "She asked if we'd be on today's stage, and when she learned we were, she wondered if we might... look out for you, so to speak."

Warmth spread through Beth's chest at the thought of Martha's continuing concern. "That's very kind, but I wouldn't want to impose—"

"Nonsense," Eleanor interrupted firmly. "It's no imposition. The journey can be difficult, and it's always better to have companions. Besides, my husband snores terribly, so I'll welcome feminine conversation to distract me."

Despite her fatigue and anxiety, Beth smiled at the woman's forthright manner. "Thank you, then. I appreciate the company."

Eleanor lowered her voice slightly. "Martha mentioned your... situation. A mail-order arrangement?"

Beth nodded, her cheeks warming.

"I won't pry," Eleanor assured her. "But if you need any advice or words of encouragement, please don't hesitate to ask." She straightened, her tone becoming brisk again. "Now, we should secure our seats. The best positions are on the left side, away from the sun's glare in the afternoon."

As they moved toward the stagecoach, Beth marveled at how, once again, providence seemed to place helpful guides in her path. First Martha, then Wilburn, now Penelope—strangers extending kindness to ease her way. Each encounter strengthened her hope that perhaps Hopewell Creek would indeed be the fresh start she sought, despite Mrs. Whitman's warning in Denver.

The stagecoach driver, a weathered man with a magnificent mustache, helped Penelope and Beth board, followed by Penelope's husband David—a quiet, scholarly-looking gentleman who acknowledged Beth with a polite nod before burying himself in a scientific journal. Six other passengers joined them, creating close quarters inside the coach.

"Next stop, Pine Hollow," the driver announced, climbing to his perch. "Then Clearwater, Hopewell Creek, and finally Winsome Valley. Two days' journey, weather permitting."

With a crack of his whip and a lurch that pressed the passengers against each other, the stage began its journey away from Colorado Springs. Beth caught a last glimpse of the station through the small window, then turned her gaze forward, toward the rugged landscape that separated her from Hopewell Creek—and her future.

The coach swayed and bounced along the rough road, heading into terrain more wild and beautiful than any Beth had ever seen. Mountains rose in majestic indifference on both sides, their slopes carpeted with pines that appeared as deep green velvet from a distance. Occasionally, the coach would round a bend to reveal vistas so breathtaking that even the most seasoned travelers fell silent in appreciation.

"First time in the high country?" Eleanor asked, noticing Beth's wide-eyed gaze.

"Yes," Beth admitted. "It's... truly breathtaking."

Eleanor smiled. "That it is. We've made this journey a dozen times, and it still leaves me in awe." She leaned closer, speaking confidentially. "Many find God more readily in these mountains than in any church. There's something about standing before such grandeur that reminds us of our proper place in creation."

Beth nodded, understanding exactly what the woman meant. The mountains, with their serene permanence and towering presence, made human concerns seem fleeting and small. Yet rather than diminishing her faith, the realization strengthened it. If God had created such majesty, surely He could guide one lonely young woman to her proper place.

As the stagecoach continued its journey westward, climbing higher into passes where snow still lingered in shadowed ravines, Beth's thoughts turned again to Hopewell Creek and the man waiting there—Henry Dobbins, whose advertisement had promised a Godly home and a respectable life. She tried to picture him, to imagine their first meeting, their life together.

Would he be kind? Patient with her inexperience in frontier ways? Would he truly be the God-fearing man he claimed, or would he prove another disappointment, like her father had become?

The questions circled in her mind as the coach swayed beneath her, carrying her ever closer to answers she both yearned for and feared. Two more days of travel, and then she would know. For now, all she could do was pray—and trust that the God who had created these magnificent mountains was guiding her path through them, toward whatever awaited her in Hopewell Creek.

Chapter 6

T he stagecoach lurched violently as the driver yanked back on the reins, sending Beth crashing against the opposite seat. Luggage shifted overhead, and passengers grabbed for handholds.

"Hopewell Creek! Last stop before Winsome Valley!" the driver bellowed from above.

Beth steadied herself, heart thundering. After five grueling days of travel, she had finally arrived. Through the small window, she glimpsed buildings lining a wide, dusty main street—her destination, at last.

Penelope Smith reached across to squeeze Beth's hand. "Well, my dear, you've reached your journey's end."

"Thank you for your companionship," Beth said, her voice catching slightly.

"Remember what we discussed," Penelope whispered. "Any man worth having will value your mind as much as your cooking."

David Smith folded his newspaper. "I wish you the best with your... arrangement, Miss Beaumont."

Beth nodded gratefully as the stagecoach door swung open. The driver extended his weathered hand to assist her down the metal steps.

"Welcome to Hopewell Creek, miss."

The moment Beth's feet touched the packed dirt of Main Street, the full weight of her situation crashed upon her. She stood alone in a strange town, about to meet the man she had would marry.

The driver tossed down her trunk, raising a small cloud of dust. "Need help getting this somewhere, miss?"

"I... no, thank you. Here is fine," Beth said.

The driver shrugged, already turning away to unload the other luggage.

Beth scanned the street, taking in her surroundings. Hopewell Creek was larger than she had imagined, with two rows of buildings stretching down a wide thoroughfare. Horses were hitched at posts along the street, and men in work clothes moved purposefully between establishments. Women in practical dresses carried baskets or shepherded children along the wooden sidewalks.

Above it all rose the white steeple of the church, gleaming against the vast Colorado sky. The sight of it eased some of Beth's anxiety. At least that part had been true.

"Ma'am? You look a mite lost."

Beth turned to find a boy of perhaps twelve years regarding her curiously.

"I'm looking for Mr. Henry Dobbins," she said. "Do you know him?"

The boy's open expression darkened slightly. "Yes'm. He lives down that way." He pointed toward the far end of town. "Past the blacksmith, white house with the broken gate."

"Thank you," Beth said, pressing a penny into his hand.

"You want me to carry your trunk?" the boy offered.

Beth hesitated. Her funds were desperately low, but the trunk was heavy. "How much would you charge?"

"Two bits," the boy said promptly.

She winced inwardly, but nodded. "Very well."

As the boy hoisted her trunk onto his shoulder with surprising strength, Beth took a steadying breath.

"Could we stop at the church first?" she asked the boy.

He shrugged. "It's your two bits."

The church stood on slightly elevated ground, making the white steeple visible from anywhere in town. As they approached, Beth noted the simple, clean lines of the building, the freshly painted clapboards, and the well-tended yard surrounding it. A sign beside the double doors read "Hopewell Creek Community Church—All Welcome—Sunday Services 10 AM—Pastor Paul Hawthorne."

"Wait here, please," Beth told the boy, who promptly sat on her trunk in the shade of a large oak tree.

The church door was unlocked, and Beth stepped into the cool interior. Sunlight filtered through modest stained-glass windows, casting colored patterns across plain wooden pews. The silence embraced her like a physical presence after days of constant stagecoach noise.

"Hello?" she called softly, her voice echoing slightly.

A door at the back of the sanctuary opened, and a tall man with graying hair and kind eyes emerged. "Good afternoon," he said, his voice warm. "I'm Pastor Paul Hawthorne. May I help you?"

Beth moved toward him, suddenly conscious of her travel-worn appearance. "I'm Elizabeth Beaumont. I've just arrived in town and..."

She faltered, uncertain how to explain her situation to a stranger, even a pastor.

"I'm looking for Mr. Henry Dobbins," she said. "I was hoping you might know where to find him."

Something flickered in Pastor Paul's eyes—concern? Wariness? It passed so quickly, Beth couldn't be certain.

"Mr. Dobbins lives at the north end of town," he said carefully. "White house with a broken fence gate. May I ask your business with him?"

The question, though gently asked, brought heat to Beth's cheeks. "I... we have an arrangement," she said vaguely.

Understanding dawned in the pastor's eyes, followed unmistakably by concern. "I see," he said, his tone measured. "Miss Beaumont, how much do you know about Mr. Dobbins?"

A cold knot formed in Beth's stomach. "He advertised for a wife in the newspaper."

Pastor Paul was silent for a long moment. "Miss Beaumont, I believe—"

"I should go meet him," Beth interrupted, suddenly desperate to escape the pity she saw forming in the pastor's eyes. "Thank you for your help. Please keep me in your prayers."

"Miss Beaumont," the pastor called as she turned to leave. "Should you need assistance of any kind, my door is always open."

Beth nodded without turning back, forcing herself to walk at a measured pace out of the church. The boy still waited on her trunk, whittling a stick.

"I'm ready to go now," she told him, struggling to keep her voice steady.

As they made their way through town toward Henry Dobbins' house, Beth felt the weight of curious glances from the townspeople. Did they know something she didn't? The pastor's concern, the boy's darkened expression—something wasn't right.

By the time they reached the white house with the broken gate, Beth's nerves were drawn tight as fiddle strings. The house itself did nothing to ease her anxiety. Though it had once been painted white, the clapboards were now gray with weathering and neglect. The front yard was overgrown, and a broken rocking chair tilted sadly on the porch.

The boy set her trunk beside the gate. "This is it," he said, almost apologetically.

Beth paid him the promised two bits, adding another penny. "Thank you for your help."

He pocketed the coins. "Thank you, ma'am," he said before darting away.

Beth stood frozen before the broken gate, trying to reconcile the dilapidated house before her with the dreams she had envisioned. Perhaps there was a mistake. Perhaps this was the wrong house.

"Lord, give me strength," she whispered, then pushed open the gate.

The creak of the hinge seemed unnaturally loud in the quiet afternoon. Beth made her way up the path, lifting her skirts slightly to avoid the weeds. At the porch steps, she hesitated again, then forced herself to climb them.

She knocked firmly on the door, smoothing her travel-rumpled skirt with damp palms as she waited.

After a long moment, the door swung open to reveal a thin woman with faded blonde hair pulled severely back from a narrow face. Her expression was unwelcoming, her posture rigid with suspicion.

"Yes?" the woman asked, her tone clipped.

"Good afternoon," Beth said, summoning a polite smile. "I'm looking for Mr. Henry Dobbins."

The woman's eyes narrowed. "What business do you have with my husband?"

The world seemed to tilt beneath Beth's feet. "Your... husband?"

"That's what I said." The woman crossed her arms. "I'm Mrs. Dobbins. Now state your business or be on your way."

Beth felt as though she'd been struck. "There must be some mistake. I'm Elizabeth Beaumont. I come regarding an ad in a newspaper... regarding marriage."

Mrs. Dobbins' expression shifted from suspicion to a cold, bitter understanding. "You too, eh?" She gave a harsh laugh. "You'd better come inside."

Numbly, Beth followed the woman into a dim, cluttered front room that smelled of stale cooking and tobacco. Mrs. Dobbins did not invite her to sit.

"You're what, the third or fourth this year?" Mrs. Dobbins said, eyeing Beth with a mixture of contempt and something almost like pity. "Henry's been placing those advertisements in papers back East for years. Says he's a lonely widower seeking a God-fearing wife." She spat the words like venom.

"I don't understand," Beth whispered, though the terrible truth was dawning on her.

"It's simple enough," Mrs. Dobbins said flatly. "My husband is a liar, a cheat, and a swindler. We've been married for fifteen years. He places those advertisements, makes promises to desperate women, gets them to send money and then come west..." She paused. "Did you send him money?"

Beth shook her head, her throat too tight for words.

"Small mercies," Mrs. Dobbins muttered.

"I never corresponded with him," Beth said, her voice barely audible. "I saw the ad, prayed for guidance, and then I came. I did send a letter when I left St. Louis letting Mr. Dobbins know I was coming..."

Mrs. Dobbins laughed again, the sound brittle and hollow.

Beth swayed slightly, gripping the back of a chair for support. Every dream, every hope she'd built over the past few days crumbled to dust. She had left everything behind, spent her last savings on this journey, all for a cruel deception.

"Where is he?" she managed to ask.

"At the saloon, most likely," Mrs. Dobbins said. "Where he spends most of his time when he's not writing his pretty lies to women like you."

A horrible thought struck Beth. "Do you allow this? These deceptions?"

Something flared in Mrs. Dobbins' eyes—anger, shame, or both. "I neither allow nor prevent it. Henry does as he pleases. Always has. I am stuck in this life and nowhere to go." She studied Beth for a moment. "You're younger than the others. Pretty, too. If you've got any sense, you'll get back on tomorrow's stage and forget you ever heard of Hopewell Creek."

The brutal practicality of the woman's advice struck Beth like a physical blow. Return to St. Louis? She had barely enough money for a night's lodging, let alone a return journey. And what would await her there? Her parents' gambling debts? The same cycle of despair she had fled?

"I can't go back," Beth whispered.

Mrs. Dobbins' expression hardened. "That's not my concern. You people come here with your dreams and your expectations, thinking the West is some kind of answer to your prayers. Well, it's not. It's just another place where people disappoint you." She moved toward the door. "Now, if you'll excuse me, I have washing to finish."

Beth remained rooted to the spot, unable to process the completeness of her situation. "What am I supposed to do now?" she asked, the question escaping before she could stop it.

Mrs. Dobbins paused at the door. For a brief moment, something like genuine sympathy crossed her face. "There's a boarding house. Mrs. Jenkins might have a room. Beyond that..." She shrugged. "That's for you to figure out."

As if in a trance, Beth walked out of the house and closed the door firmly behind her. The afternoon sun beat down mercilessly, the dusty street stretching out before her with brutal indifference to her plight.

Her trunk still sat at the gate, containing everything she owned in the world. Beyond it lay a town she didn't know, filled with people who were strangers, and no means to return to the life she had left behind.

The enormity of her situation crashed over her like a wave. She had been deceived, betrayed in the cruelest way. She was utterly alone, nearly penniless, stranded in a frontier town hundreds of miles from anything familiar.

Beth sank onto the porch step, no longer able to maintain the composure that had carried her through the dreadful conversation. Hot tears spilled down her cheeks as the full weight of her predicament settled upon her shoulders.

"Oh God," she whispered, her voice breaking. "What have I done?"

For the first time since leaving St. Louis, Beth allowed herself to weep openly, her shoulders shaking with silent sobs. Everything—the long journey, the hope she had carried, the desperate gamble for a better life—all of it had been for nothing. Worse than nothing, for at least in St. Louis she had known what to expect.

She didn't know how long she sat there, weeping on a stranger's porch step. Eventually, the sound of approaching footsteps roused her. Hastily wiping her eyes, Beth looked up to see a man striding purposefully toward the house, his expression darkening as he spotted her.

He was of medium height, wiry rather than stout, with a mustache that did little to hide the mean set of his mouth. His clothes were rumpled, and even from a distance, Beth could smell the whiskey on him.

She knew, with sickening certainty, that this was Henry Dobbins.

"Who the devil are you?" he demanded, stopping at the broken gate.

Beth rose on unsteady legs, summoning the last shreds of her dignity. "Elizabeth Beaumont."

Recognition and wariness flickered in his bloodshot eyes. "Beaumont?" he repeated, clearly searching his memory.

"I came here regarding your ad. I sent you a letter days ago when I left St. Louis," Beth said, her voice steadier than she felt.

Dobbins cursed under his breath. "Foolish girl."

The casual dismissal in his tone rekindled something in Beth—not hope, but a spark of the righteous anger that had been smothered beneath her shock and grief.

"I met your wife," she said, descending the porch steps to stand before him.

Dobbins's expression hardened. "Look, girl, I don't know what you thought was going to happen here—"

"You deceived me. You lied in your ad," Beth interrupted, her voice rising.

People were beginning to take notice. A woman looked out her window across the street. Two men outside a home nearby turned to watch.

"Keep your voice down," Dobbins hissed, glancing around nervously.

"Why should I?" Beth demanded, beyond caring about propriety or discretion.

Dobbins grabbed her arm, his fingers digging painfully into her flesh. "I said, be quiet," he growled.

Beth wrenched her arm free, stepping back. "Don't touch me. You have no right."

"You little fool," Dobbins spat. "You think anyone here cares about your wounded feelings? This isn't some civilized Eastern city. This is the frontier. People do what they must to survive."

"Deception and cruelty aren't survival," Beth retorted. "They're sin, plain and simple. And I won't be silent about it."

Dobbins's face darkened with rage. For a terrible moment, Beth thought he might strike her, right there in the street. Instead, he stepped back.

"Get off my property," he said coldly. "And take your trunk with you. I don't care where you go or what happens to you. You are a crazy woman for coming here without waiting for a response from me."

With that, he pushed past her and stormed into the house, slamming the door behind him.

Beth stood trembling in the yard, acutely aware of the curious stares from passersby. She had stood her ground, but at what cost? She was now truly stranded, with nowhere to go and night approaching.

Her legs threatened to buckle beneath her. Blindly, she made her way to her trunk and sank down upon it, fighting back a fresh wave of tears. She would not break down again, not here in the street where anyone could see.

Chapter 7

"Miss? Are you all right?"

The voice was deep and concerned. Beth looked up to find one of the men from across the street standing before her. Up close, she could see he was perhaps in his late twenties, tall and broad-shouldered, with intelligent hazel eyes that studied her with genuine concern.

"I'm fine," she managed, the lie transparent even to her own ears.

He didn't contradict her, for which she was grateful. Instead, he said simply, "I'm Ezra Simmons, editor of the Hopewell Creek Herald."

"Elizabeth Beaumont," she replied automatically.

"Miss Beaumont," he said, his tone careful, "I couldn't help but overhear some of what just transpired. It seems you find yourself in difficult circumstances."

Beth glanced toward the house, where the curtain twitched in the front window. Mrs. Dobbins was watching.

"You could say that," Beth admitted, her voice barely audible.

Ezra Simmons followed her gaze, his expression hardening momentarily before returning to careful neutrality. "Do you have somewhere to go? Friends or family in town, perhaps?"

Beth shook her head, ashamed to admit the full extent of her predicament to this stranger. "I was told there might be a room at a boarding house. Mrs. Jenkins, I believe."

"Mrs. Jenkins does indeed run a respectable boarding house," Ezra confirmed. "But, if I may be so bold—do you have the means to secure lodging?"

The direct question, though gently asked, brought fresh heat to Beth's cheeks. "I have some funds," she said vaguely, unwilling to admit how pitifully small they were.

Something in Ezra's expression suggested he understood more than she was saying, but he didn't press the point. Instead, he reached down and grasped the handle of her trunk.

"Allow me to escort you to Mrs. Jenkins's establishment," he said firmly. "It's not far, but the streets can be confusing for newcomers."

Beth hesitated. What choice did she have? She was alone in an unfamiliar town, with night approaching and no prospects.

"Thank you," she said finally. "That's very kind."

As they walked away from the Dobbins' house, Beth felt the stares following them. What must they think—the newcomer woman, walking with a man, her face tear-streaked and her composure in tatters?

"You shouldn't trouble yourself," she said quietly as they turned onto a side street. "I'm sure people will talk."

Ezra glanced down at her, a hint of dry humor touching his lips. "Miss Beaumont, I run the town newspaper. People always talk about me."

Despite everything, Beth felt a ghost of a smile touch her lips.

They walked in silence for a moment before Ezra spoke again. "I won't pry into your affairs, Miss Beaumont, but if there's been some kind of deception or wrongdoing, it might be worth discussing."

Beth kept her eyes on the path ahead. "What makes you think that?"

"I'm a newspaperman," he said simply. "It's my job to observe, to listen between the words people say. And what I observed just now was a young woman of obvious good character in distress, and Henry Dobbins—a man known to me by reputation—behaving in a manner that suggests he's caused that distress."

Beth swallowed hard. "You know Mr. Dobbins?"

"Not personally, no. But in a town this size, reputation travels quickly." He paused. "As does word of certain patterns of behavior."

"What do you mean?" Beth asked, though part of her already knew.

Ezra stopped walking, turning to face her fully. "Miss Beaumont, you're not the first woman to arrive in Hopewell Creek expecting to marry Henry Dobbins. There have been others."

"I am a fool," she said bitterly.

"You are not," Ezra corrected gently. "Dobbins is not a good man. The women he summons usually leave town quickly, ashamed or threatened into silence. The few who have spoken out have found themselves disbelieved or dismissed as jilted and vindictive."

"And what do you believe, Mr. Simmons?" Beth asked, meeting his gaze directly for the first time.

Ezra held her eyes for a long moment. "I believe Henry Dobbins is a con man who preys on vulnerable women, Miss Beaumont. I also believe that if someone were willing to speak out—someone of obvious character and integrity—it might put a stop to his schemes."

"No one would believe me, a stranger, over an established resident."

"Some might not," Ezra acknowledged. "But others would. I would."

The simple declaration startled Beth. "You don't even know me."

"I know what I observed," Ezra said firmly. "And I know my own mind, Miss Beaumont. But," he added, his tone softening, "this isn't a decision you need to make now. First, let's secure you proper lodging."

They resumed walking, turning onto a street lined with modest but well-kept houses. Ezra stopped before one painted a cheerful yellow, with a small but tidy garden in front.

"This is Mrs. Jenkins' boarding house," he said. "She's a good woman, fair and discreet."

Beth stared at the house, her courage faltering. What would she say? How could she explain her situation without revealing the whole humiliating truth? And even if Mrs. Jenkins took pity on her, how long could her meager funds last?

"Mr. Simmons," she said, her voice barely above a whisper, "I should tell you that my circumstances are... limited. I don't know how long I can afford lodging, or what I'll do after that."

Ezra set down her trunk, considering her words. "Miss Beaumont, I may have a proposition for you if you're willing to hear it."

Beth tensed. She had already been deceived by one man's "proposition" in this town.

Sensing her wariness, Ezra continued quickly, "It's a matter of business, nothing more. My assistant at the newspaper recently left her position—she's expecting a child and has returned to her family. I find myself in need of someone who can read, write, and learn the basics of typesetting and printing. The position includes a modest salary that would cover your lodging and basic needs while you... determine your next steps."

Beth stared at him, uncertain whether to trust this unexpected offer. "Why would you offer such a position to a complete stranger?"

"Because I need help," Ezra said simply. "The newspaper doesn't run itself, and I've been working twelve-hour days trying to keep up. And because," he added with a slight smile, "anyone who stands up to Henry Dobbins in the middle of the street has the kind of courage I value in an employee."

Despite everything, Beth felt a flicker of genuine amusement at his reasoning. "I'm not certain that was courage, Mr. Simmons. It might have been foolishness."

"Sometimes they're the same thing," he replied. "Will you consider it?"

Beth hesitated. The offer was unexpected, perhaps heaven-sent. Yet, she had already trusted too easily over the past several days.

"You don't have to decide immediately," Ezra said, noting her hesitation. "Take the night to pray about it if you wish. In the meantime, let me introduce you to Mrs. Jenkins."

The front door of the boarding house opened, and a plump, gray-haired woman emerged onto the porch.

"Ezra Simmons, is that you lurking at my gate?" she called, her tone affectionately scolding. "Do come in instead of standing about in the street."

Ezra smiled. "Good afternoon, Mrs. Jenkins. I've brought a potential boarder for you to meet."

The woman's keen eyes shifted to Beth, taking in her travel-worn appearance and the trunk at her feet. "Well, don't keep the poor girl standing in the heat. Bring her in, bring her in."

As Mrs. Jenkins ushered them into a cool, tidy foyer, Beth felt a wave of exhaustion crash over her. The emotional turmoil of the day, combined with the physical strain of the journey, left her dizzy and disoriented.

Ezra must have noticed, for he said quickly, "Mrs. Jenkins, this is Miss Elizabeth Beaumont, newly arrived from St. Louis. She's had a long journey and has experienced some... unexpected complications upon arrival. She unfortunately met Mr. Dobbins just now. I believe she could use a cup of tea and a quiet room, if you have one available."

Mrs. Jenkins studied Beth's face, her shrewd eyes softening with maternal concern. "Of course, I have a room. And more than tea, by the looks of it. When did you last eat a proper meal, girl?"

"Yesterday," Beth admitted, the directness of the question bypassing her usual reserve.

"Just as I thought," Mrs. Jenkins tutted. "Well, you're in luck. I've stew on the stove and biscuits in the oven. Ezra, bring the young lady's trunk to the blue room—it's vacant and has the morning sun." She turned back to Beth. "Now, dear, come with me to the kitchen while Ezra handles your things."

Beth allowed herself to be led through a comfortably furnished sitting room into a large, warm kitchen filled with the savory aroma of beef stew. Mrs. Jenkins guided her to a chair at the table, then busied herself at the stove.

"I'm obliged for your kindness," Beth said, finding her voice at last. "But I should tell you that my funds are limited. I can pay for tonight, but beyond that..."

Mrs. Jenkins waved a dismissive hand. "We'll discuss payment later. First, you'll eat and rest."

Ezra appeared in the doorway. "Your trunk is in the room, Miss Beaumont. Mrs. Jenkins will show you upstairs when you're ready." He hesitated. "About my offer—the newspaper office is on Main Street in town. You can't miss it. If you're interested, come by tomorrow morning around eight. If not..." He shrugged. "No harm in asking."

"Thank you," Beth said, the words inadequate for the lifeline he had extended. "I'll consider it carefully."

After Ezra departed, Mrs. Jenkins placed a steaming bowl of stew and a golden biscuit before Beth. "Eat," she instructed firmly. "Then we'll talk."

The simple kindness—warm food, a gentle tone, the absence of prying questions—broke through the last of Beth's composure. Tears welled in her eyes, spilling over before she could stop them.

"I'm sorry," she said, hastily wiping them away. "It's been a difficult day."

Mrs. Jenkins sat down across from her, her expression compassionate but practical. "I imagine it has, coming all this way to find Henry Dobbins already married."

Beth's head snapped up. "How did you know?"

The older woman's expression softened further. "Dear girl, you're not the first. I assume what must have brought you here. Ezra mentioned Mr. Dobbins, remember. Three other girls have sat at this very table, just as shocked and heartbroken as you are now."

"Three?" Beth repeated, horrified. "And nothing has been done to stop him?"

Mrs. Jenkins sighed. "What can be done? It's not illegal to place ads full of false promises. The others left town quickly, too ashamed to stay. One had a family she could return to. The others..." she trailed off, her expression troubled.

"What happened to them?" Beth asked, though she feared the answer.

"I heard one took work in a saloon in Denver," Mrs. Jenkins whispered. "The other, I never knew. She left in the night without a word. I've often prayed she found her way to somewhere kind."

The weight of other women's shattered dreams pressed upon Beth, adding to her own burden of despair.

"I can't go back," she said, more to herself than to Mrs. Jenkins. "And I won't..." She couldn't bring herself to finish the sentence, to acknowledge the desperate choices that might await her.

"No one's asking you to do either," Mrs. Jenkins said firmly. "Eat your stew, child. Things often look clearer after a good meal and a night's rest."

Beth obediently took a spoonful of the rich stew, realizing as she did how desperately hungry she was.

When Beth had eaten her fill and color had returned to her cheeks, Mrs. Jenkins spoke again. "Would you like to tell me what happened?"

Beth hesitated. She barely knew this woman, kind as she seemed. Yet, keeping the whole painful truth bottled inside felt unbearable.

Haltingly at first, then with increasing fluency, Beth told Mrs. Jenkins everything—her parents' gambling addiction, her brother's death, the desperate decision to answer Henry's advertisement, the journey west, and finally, the devastating revelation upon arrival.

"I was such a fool," she concluded, fresh tears threatening. "I believed everything in the ad because I wanted so desperately for it to be true."

"That doesn't make you a fool, child," Mrs. Jenkins said gently. "It makes you human. We all want to believe the best, especially when the alternative is too painful to consider."

A knock at the kitchen door interrupted their conversation. Mrs. Jenkins rose to answer it, blocking Beth's view of the visitor.

"Is she here?" a woman's voice asked quietly.

"She is," Mrs. Jenkins replied, equally quiet. "Exhausted and heart-broken, poor thing."

"I thought as much," the woman said. "I've brought these from the church donation box."

Mrs. Jenkins accepted what appeared to be a bundle of clothing. "That's kind of you, Mary. I'll see she gets them."

After the visitor departed, Mrs. Jenkins returned to the table with a small stack of neatly folded garments—three simple day dresses, a nightgown, and some essential undergarments.

"The pastor's wife," she explained, placing them before Beth. "Don't worry, neither of us is one to gossip. These aren't new, but they're clean and well-made and by the looks of your small trunk, you didn't bring much."

Beth touched the simple cotton dress on top of the pile, over-whelmed by the thoughtfulness of the gesture. "I can't accept—"

"You can, and you will," Mrs. Jenkins interrupted firmly. "Pride is a luxury for those with options, my girl. Besides, these were given to the church specifically to help those in need. Would you deny someone the blessing of giving?"

Put that way, Beth could hardly refuse. "Thank you," she said simply. "Please thank Mrs.—"

"Hawthorne. Mary Hawthorne, the pastor's wife. And you can thank her yourself on Sunday." Mrs. Jenkins stood, gathering their dishes. "Now, I expect you'd like to wash away the dust of travel and rest a bit. I'll show you to your room."

The "blue room," as Mrs. Jenkins called it, was small but immac-ulately clean, with a narrow iron bed covered by a patchwork quilt, a washstand with basin and pitcher, a simple wooden chair, and a small wardrobe. A window overlooked a kitchen garden at the back of the house.

"The washroom is at the end of the hall," Mrs. Jenkins explained. "You'll share it with two other boarders—both respectable older ladies who work at the millinery shop."

"You're very kind," Beth said, meaning it deeply.

Mrs. Jenkins patted her shoulder. "Get some rest, dear. Things often look brighter after sleep."

Left alone, Beth sank onto the edge of the bed, still struggling to process the dramatic reversal of her fortunes. This morning, she had awakened on the stagecoach full of anticipation for her new life. Now, that dream lay shattered at her feet, replaced by an uncertain future in a strange town.

Chapter 8

Beth woke before dawn, her eyes snapping open in the unfamiliar room. For a disorienting moment, she couldn't remember where she was. Then yesterday's events rushed back—Henry Dobbins' deception, her humiliation in the street, and the unexpected kindness of strangers.

She sat up, drawing the patchwork quilt around her shoulders against the morning chill. Through the window, the sky was just beginning to lighten, transforming from inky black to deep purple.

Beth's stomach clenched with anxiety as she contemplated the newspaper job Mr. Simmons had offered. Could she truly manage such work? She had always been a quick learner, but typesetting and printing were trades she knew nothing about. Yet, what choice did she have? Her funds were low.

"Lord," she whispered, her voice tentative in the quiet room, "I don't understand why You've brought me here, to this place, in these circumstances. But I trust You have a purpose." The prayer felt rusty on her lips after months of neglecting her faith, but somehow right.

Beth rose and dressed in one of the donated dresses. It was a simple calico, a bit loose but clean and serviceable, and prettier than the dresses she had brought with her. She washed her face in the basin, pinned her honey-blonde hair into a practical knot, and tried to compose herself for whatever the day might bring.

When she ventured downstairs, Mrs. Jenkins was already in the kitchen, kneading bread dough with strong, flour-dusted hands.

"Good morning, dear," the older woman greeted her. "You're up early. Did you sleep?"

"Some," Beth admitted. "I'm going to visit the newspaper office this morning. Mr. Simmons offered me work."

Mrs. Jenkins nodded approvingly. "Ezra's a good man. Honest to a fault. The most trustworthy fellow in Hopewell Creek, if you ask me."

"That is good to know," Beth said, accepting the cup of coffee Mrs. Jenkins poured.

"I've known him since he was knee high to a grasshopper," Mrs. Jenkins replied, returning to her dough. "His parents are good people too—stalwart members of the church. His father runs the most prosperous cattle ranch in the county, and his mother taught school before her health declined." She punched the dough with particular vigor. "Ezra could have stayed on the ranch, had an easier life, but he had a hankering for words and ideas. Bought the newspaper five years ago when old Mr. Thatcher retired."

Beth sipped her coffee, absorbing this information. "Does he have a family of his own? A wife?" she asked casually, telling herself it was merely practical to know more about her potential employer.

"No wife yet, though not for lack of interested parties," Mrs. Jenkins said with a knowing look. "That Rosalind Fairfield—banker's daughter—has been setting her cap for him since she returned from that fancy boarding school back East. All fluttery eyelashes and simpering smiles whenever he's about."

Beth kept her expression neutral, though she noted the disapproval in Mrs. Jenkins' tone. "I see."

"Mmm. She sees him as a prize to be won, I expect. Status and all that nonsense. Ezra deserves better—someone who values his character, not his position." Mrs. Jenkins slapped the dough into a greased bowl and covered it with a cloth. "But that's neither here nor there. You'll need sustenance before you start your day. Sit down and I'll fix you some breakfast."

Despite Beth's protests that she wasn't hungry, Mrs. Jenkins soon placed a plate of fried eggs, bacon, and a thick slice of yesterday's bread before her. "Eat," she commanded. "You'll need your strength."

By the time Beth finished breakfast and helped Mrs. Jenkins wash the dishes, it was nearly seven-thirty. She gathered her courage, thanked her hostess, and set out for Main Street with directions to the Herald office clutched in her hand.

Hopewell Creek was beginning to stir as Beth walked briskly through the streets. Shopkeepers swept their boardwalks, the blacksmith's forge was already smoking, and wagons rolled past carrying goods or farmers coming to town for supplies. Several people nodded politely as she passed, but no one stopped her. For that, Beth was grateful. She wasn't ready for questions.

She found the newspaper office easily enough—a sturdy wooden building with large windows showcasing a sign that read "Hopewell Creek Herald" in bold letters. Beth hesitated on the boardwalk, her heart racing. Through the window, she could see movement inside—a tall figure adjusting something on a large machine that must be the printing press.

Ezra Simmons. Her potential employer. The man who had extended a lifeline when she was drowning in despair.

Before she could talk herself out of it, Beth squared her shoulders, took a deep breath, and pushed open the door.

Ezra looked up from the press, his face registering surprise and then a warm smile that crinkled the corners of his hazel eyes. "Miss Beaumont," he said, wiping his ink-stained hands on a rag. "Good morning. You came."

"Eight o'clock, as you suggested," Beth replied, standing awkwardly just inside the door. "I hope I'm not interrupting your work."

"Not at all," Ezra said, gesturing for her to come further into the office. "I'm just making some adjustments to the press. There's always something that needs tinkering with."

Beth stepped forward, taking in the bustling organized chaos of the newspaper office. The air smelled of ink, paper, and the faint metallic scent of the type pieces. The main room was dominated by the printing press—a complex machine with gears, levers, and a flat bed where papers would be printed. Along one wall stood rows of wooden cases filled with metal type pieces—tiny letters, numbers, and punctuation marks sorted into compartments. A large desk, presumably Ezra's, occupied a corner near the window, piled high with papers, books, and writing implements.

The space was utilitarian, but not unwelcoming. A pot-bellied stove in the corner gave off welcome heat against the morning chill, and someone—Ezra, she presumed—had placed a vase of wildflowers on a small table near the entrance.

"It's quite an operation," Beth said, genuinely impressed.

"It keeps me busy," Ezra agreed. He gestured to a chair near his desk. "Please, sit down. I imagine you have questions about the position."

Beth sat, arranging her skirts carefully. "Yes. I should be honest, Mr. Simmons. I have no experience with newspaper work. I can read and write well enough, but typesetting and printing are entirely foreign to me."

Ezra settled into his own chair, his expression thoughtful. "Most skills can be taught, Miss Beaumont. What can't be taught are character and intelligence, both of which you appear to possess in abundance."

Beth felt heat rise to her cheeks at the unexpected compliment. "That's kind of you to say, but you hardly know me."

"True enough," Ezra acknowledged with a slight smile. "Let's remedy that. Tell me about yourself—your background, your education, your experience. Whatever you're comfortable sharing."

Beth hesitated. How much should she reveal? Her family's shameful decline? The desperate circumstances that had driven her to answer Henry Dobbins' advertisement?

"I was raised in St. Louis," she began cautiously. "My parents ensured I received a good education—reading, writing, mathematics, history, and a little French and music. I had planned to become a teacher before..."

"Before circumstances altered your path," Ezra supplied when she faltered.

"Yes." Beth was grateful for his tact. "I've had no formal employment, but I managed our household for the past few years—maintaining accounts, correspondence, and practical matters."

"And what brought you to Hopewell Creek?" Ezra asked gently, but Beth tensed nonetheless.

"Henry Dobbins' advertisement. A new start seemed... necessary at the time."

Ezra leaned forward, his expression serious. "Miss Beaumont, I hope you understand that I'm not asking out of idle curiosity. If you come to work here, people will ask questions. Some will already have heard you arrived expecting to marry Henry Dobbins. Others will speculate. I'd like to know how you wish to address such inquiries."

Beth appreciated his directness. "I have nothing to hide, Mr. Simmons. I answered Mr. Dobbins' advertisement in good faith, arrived to find him already married, and now find myself in need of employment. Those are the facts. I won't embellish them or hide them."

A look of approval crossed Ezra's face. "That's an admirable approach. Straightforward and honest."

"The truth has a way of emerging eventually," Beth said. "I learned that lesson watching my parents try to conceal our... difficulties."

Ezra nodded, though Beth sensed his curiosity about what "difficulties" she referred to. To his credit, he didn't press for details.

"Well then," he continued, "allow me to explain what the position entails. The Herald publishes on Wednesdays. I write most of the articles myself, though we occasionally have contributions from townspeople for special events or topics."

He gestured around the office. "Marjorie, my previous assistant, helped with typesetting, proofreading, and the actual printing process. She also managed subscriptions, took classified advertisements, and kept our accounts in order." He smiled ruefully. "It's a fair amount of work, as you can see. I've been managing alone since she left weeks ago, which is... challenging."

"I can imagine," Beth said, noting the shadows beneath his eyes that suggested long hours.

"The position pays fifteen dollars a week, which should cover your board at Mrs. Jenkins' with some left over," Ezra continued. "Hours are generally eight to five, though on printing days, we sometimes work later. Sunday, of course, is for rest and worship."

Fifteen dollars a week! Beth tried to keep her expression neutral, but inwardly she was astonished at the generosity of the offer. It was more than she had dared hope for.

"That's very fair," she managed to say.

Ezra studied her for a moment. "Do you have any questions for me, Miss Beaumont?"

"How soon would you want me to start? And what would my first tasks be?" Beth asked practically.

"Today, if you're willing," Ezra said. "We print tomorrow's edition this afternoon. I could show you the basics of typesetting this morning—it's detailed work that requires patience and precision, qualities I suspect you possess."

Beth felt a flutter of nervousness, but nodded. "I'm willing to try."

"Excellent," Ezra said, standing. "There's one more matter we should discuss before you accept." His tone became more serious. "As I mentioned yesterday, Henry Dobbins has employed this scheme before. I believe it's wrong and should be stopped. If you're amenable, I'd like to run a story in the Herald, exposing his actions. Nothing that would embarrass you personally—just the facts about his deceptive advertisements and pattern of behavior."

Beth blinked in surprise. "You would do that?"

"With your permission, yes. It's a matter of public interest—protecting other women from similar deception. And frankly, it's the right thing to do." Ezra's eyes held a steely determination that Beth found oddly reassuring. "Dobbins won't like it, of course. He might even threaten legal action, though he'd have no grounds. But you should be aware that publishing such a story could create some... discomfort."

Beth considered this. The thought of having her name associated with such a scandal—even as a victim—was daunting. Yet, the alternative—allowing Henry Dobbins to continue preying on vulnerable women—was unconscionable.

"What of Mrs. Dobbins?" she asked. "Would such a story cause her public humiliation?"

Ezra's expression softened. "Your concern for her speaks well of your character, Miss Beaumont. I intend to speak with Mrs. Dobbins privately before publishing anything. From what I've gathered, she's aware of her husband's activities but feels powerless to stop them. She might even welcome the exposure."

Beth nodded slowly. "Then yes, you have my permission. If it might prevent another woman from experiencing what I have, it's worth any discomfort to me."

"Thank you," Ezra said simply. "Your courage does you credit." He cleared his throat, as if momentarily disconcerted by the intensity of the moment. "Now, shall we begin your training? The sooner you learn the basics, the sooner you'll feel useful."

"Yes, please," Beth said, rising from her chair with renewed determination. This chance—this opportunity to rebuild her life with dignity and purpose—felt like a gift she couldn't quite believe. "I'm eager to learn."

Ezra led her to the wall of type cases. "This is where we begin—with the letters themselves. Every word that appears in the Herald starts here."

For the next hour, Ezra patiently explained the fundamentals of typesetting. The wooden cases were organized with a specific logic—capital letters in the upper case, lowercase letters in the lower case (thus the terms, Beth realized), with the most commonly used letters placed for easy access. Each tiny metal letter had to be placed backwards in the composing stick, reading from left to right but inverted, so that when inked and pressed to paper, it would appear correctly.

"It takes practice," Ezra assured her when she fumbled, dropping several letters that scattered across the floor. "Marjorie broke an entire line of type her first day. We were finding letters under the press for weeks."

Beth laughed despite herself. "That makes me feel slightly better."

They worked side by side, Ezra demonstrating and Beth practicing, setting a simple classified advertisement for Bellwether's Blacksmith Shop. Her fingers grew more confident as she worked, and when she completed the short notice correctly, she felt a surprising sense of accomplishment.

"Well done," Ezra said, examining her work. "You have steady hands and a good eye for detail. Those are essential qualities in this work."

Beth tried not to appear too pleased at his praise. "It's interesting work. More complex than I expected."

"Many people think newspapers simply appear, with little thought to the process behind them," Ezra said, carefully placing the completed advertisement on a tray. "Each letter, each word, each sentence must be deliberately chosen and physically placed. It teaches one to value clarity and precision."

They continued working, Ezra setting the type for a longer article while Beth practiced with another simple notice. The mechanical nature of the task was soothing, allowing Beth's mind to settle after the emotional turmoil of the previous day.

Around mid-morning, the bell above the door jingled, and both looked up to see a young woman enter the office. She was fashionably dressed in a deep burgundy visiting gown, her dark hair arranged in an elaborate style beneath a small hat adorned with silk flowers. Her vivid blue eyes immediately fixed on Ezra, her full lips curving into a dazzling smile.

"Ezra, darling!" she exclaimed, sweeping into the room like a perfumed breeze. "I was just passing by and thought I'd see how you're faring without poor Marjorie." Her gaze slid to Beth, assessing her with cool precision. "But I see you have... assistance."

"Good morning, Rosalind," Ezra said, his tone polite but noticeably cooler than when he'd spoken to Beth. "Yes, this is Miss Elizabeth Beaumont, newly arrived in Hopewell Creek. Miss Beaumont, may I present Miss Rosalind Fairfield."

Beth inclined her head politely. "Miss Fairfield."

"Miss Beaumont," Rosalind echoed, her smile not quite reaching her eyes. "How fortunate for you to find employment so quickly after arriving in our little town. One might almost call it... providential."

The slight emphasis on the last word carried an insinuation that made Beth's cheeks warm. Before she could respond, Ezra spoke.

"Indeed it is," he said firmly. "Miss Beaumont has excellent qualifications, and the Herald was in pressing need of an assistant. A fortunate circumstance for us both."

Rosalind's smile tightened almost imperceptibly. "How delightful. And where are you staying, Miss Beaumont? Hopewell Creek has so few appropriate accommodations for a young woman."

"Mrs. Jenkins has kindly provided me with a room," Beth answered, maintaining her composure despite the woman's thinly veiled hostility.

"Ah, the boarding house. Of course." Rosalind turned her attention back to Ezra. "Father mentioned he needs to speak with you about the bank's quarterly notice. Perhaps you could join us for dinner this evening? Mother is making her famous pot roast."

Ezra shook his head. "Please thank your mother for the invitation, but I'm afraid I must decline. Today is press day—Miss Beaumont and I will be working quite late, finalizing tomorrow's edition."

"I see." Rosalind's voice cooled noticeably. "Another time, then." She moved toward the door, her skirts rustling elegantly. "Do remember that the town dance is just two weeks away. You promised to escort me, Ezra."

"Did I?" Ezra's expression remained neutral. "I don't recall making any specific commitments, Rosalind."

"Well, everyone simply assumes..." she trailed off, glancing at Beth with barely concealed irritation. "We can discuss it later. Good day, Ezra. Miss Beaumont."

The bell jingled again as she departed, leaving behind the faint scent of expensive perfume and an awkward silence.

"I apologize for Miss Fairfield," Ezra said after a moment. "She can be... forward."

"There's no need to apologize," Beth said, returning her attention to the type case. "She seems quite... devoted to you."

Ezra sighed. "Rosalind and I grew up together. Her father and mine have been friends for years. I think she's decided that makes us... inevitable."

"And you don't agree?" The question slipped out before Beth could stop herself. She immediately regretted it. "I'm sorry—that's none of my business."

"No, it's a fair question, considering she just made it very much your business," Ezra said with a rueful smile. "No, I don't agree with Rosalind's assessment. She's an accomplished young woman with many admirable qualities, but..." He paused, searching for words. "We don't share the same values or vision for life. I believe marriage should be founded on deeper commonalities than social compatibility."

Beth nodded, unexpectedly touched by his sincerity. "That's a wise perspective."

"My father says I'm too particular," Ezra admitted with a slight laugh. "Perhaps he's right. But I've seen too many unions based on convenience or social advantage that bring little true happiness." He cleared his throat, suddenly seeming to realize how personal the conversation had become. "But we have work to do. Shall we continue with your training?"

"Of course," Beth agreed, grateful for the return to professional territory.

The rest of the morning passed quickly as Ezra showed Beth the various components of the newspaper—the front page always featuring the most significant local news, the middle sections for community announcements, and the back page for advertisements and classifieds. He explained the process of planning each edition, gathering news, and verifying facts.

"A newspaper has a sacred trust with its readers," he told her earnestly. "They rely on us for truth, for accuracy. It's a responsibility I take very seriously."

"As you should," Beth agreed. "Words have power."

Ezra looked at her appraisingly. "Yes, they do. I'm glad you understand that."

At midday, Ezra insisted on breaking for lunch. "There's a small cafe two doors down that serves excellent sandwiches. I usually have something sent over on busy days."

"That would be fine," Beth said, suddenly realizing how hungry she was. The morning's work, though not physically demanding, had required intense concentration.

Ezra stepped outside briefly and returned to report that lunch would arrive shortly. "In the meantime," he said, "tell me what you think of Hopewell Creek—your first impressions, limited though they may be."

Beth considered her answer carefully. "It seems a pleasant enough town, despite my unfortunate introduction to it. The people I've met have been unexpectedly kind. Mrs. Jenkins, Pastor Hawthorne and his wife, you..." She paused. "I expected a rougher, more primitive place, to be honest."

"We've grown considerably in recent years," Ezra said. "The railroad's expansion has brought new settlers, new businesses. We're still small by eastern standards, but we have most amenities a community needs—church, school, doctor, businesses." Pride was evident in his voice. "My father likes to say Hopewell Creek is poised between the wildness of the frontier and the civilization of the future. I think he's right."

Their lunch arrived—thick sandwiches of sliced beef and cheese on fresh bread, accompanied by pickles and apples—delivered by a cheerful young woman who regarded Beth with friendly curiosity.

"You must be Miss Beaumont," she said, setting down their meal. "I'm Maggie O'Leary. My parents run the general store across the street."

"Pleased to meet you," Beth replied, warming to the girl's open manner.

"Ezra mentioned you were working at the Herald now when he placed the lunch order," Maggie continued. "That's wonderful! Ezra's been run ragged since Marjorie left." She gave Ezra a fond, teasing look. "He's terrible at asking for help, you know. Stubbornly independent."

"I'm sitting right here, Maggie," Ezra said dryly, though his expression was good-natured.

"And denying none of it, I notice," Maggie retorted with a grin. She turned back to Beth. "We should have tea sometime. There aren't many young single women in Hopewell Creek. It would be nice to have a new friend."

The simple, genuine offer of friendship touched Beth unexpectedly. "I'd like that very much."

"Wonderful! I'll come by the boarding house some evening soon." With a cheerful wave, Maggie departed, leaving Beth with a warmer feeling about her prospects in Hopewell Creek.

"Maggie is a force of nature," Ezra commented as they began eating. "But she has a good heart."

"She seems lovely," Beth agreed. "Has she lived here long?"

"All her life. Her parents were among the first settlers." Ezra took a bite of his sandwich, then added, "The O'Leary's are good people. Salt of the earth. Their general store and the cafe, both of which they own, are the lifeblood of the community."

They ate in companionable silence for a few minutes, Beth savoring the simple but delicious meal. It had been a long time since she'd had regular, satisfying meals. Her parents' financial difficulties had meant increasingly sparse provisions over the past year.

"I was thinking," Ezra said, breaking the silence, "that we might run a column in the Herald about life in the East, comparing it to western living. Many of our readers are curious about the lifestyle they left behind, or some never experienced. Your perspective as a newcomer could be valuable."

Beth looked up in surprise. "You want me to write for the newspaper?"

"Eventually, yes. Not immediately—you'll need time to settle in and learn the mechanics of production first. But from our conversations this morning, it's clear you have a thoughtful, articulate mind. That's a valuable asset for a newspaper."

"I've never written for publication," Beth admitted, both flattered and daunted by the suggestion.

"You wouldn't need to at first. We could start with your observations, which I could shape into articles. Over time, as you become more comfortable, you might take on more of the writing yourself."

His confidence in her abilities, based on such limited acquaintance, was both bewildering and heartening. "I'd be willing to try," she said cautiously.

Ezra smiled, the expression warming his normally serious features and crinkling the corners of his eyes. "Excellent. We'll start slowly."

After lunch, Ezra introduced Beth to the printing press itself—an intimidating iron machine with numerous levers, rollers, and moving parts. He explained how the type was arranged in frames called chases, how ink was applied to the type using rollers, and how paper was pressed against the inked type to create the printed page.

"It's a mechanical miracle, really," he said, his enthusiasm evident as he demonstrated the process. "Gutenberg's invention revolutionized the spread of knowledge. What once took scribes months to copy can now be reproduced hundreds of times in a single day."

"It's remarkable," Beth agreed, watching as he operated the press with practiced ease. "Though I imagine I'll need considerable practice before I'm trusted with this part of the process."

"Indeed," Ezra said with a chuckle. "The press can be temperamental. It took me months to master all its quirks."

Throughout the afternoon, various townspeople dropped by the Herald office—some to place advertisements, others to share news items, and a few seemingly just to satisfy their curiosity about the new arrival. Ezra introduced Beth to each visitor with a simple explanation that she was his new assistant, recently arrived from St. Louis. To her relief, no one asked direct questions about her connection to Henry Dobbins, though she sensed underlying curiosity in some glances.

As the day progressed, Beth found herself settling into a rhythm—learning tasks, asking questions when necessary, observing Ezra's methodical approach to newspaper production. Despite her initial nervousness, the work was engaging, even satisfying. For the first time since arriving in Hopewell Creek, she felt purposeful rather than adrift.

Chapter 9

Around four o'clock, Ezra asked Beth to proofread his main article—a piece about a proposed expansion of the school building.

"Fresh eyes are invaluable," he said, handing her the galley proof. "I often miss my own errors because I know what I intended to write."

Beth seated herself at the small desk Ezra had cleared for her use and began reading carefully, marking a few minor errors with a pencil. The article was clear, well-reasoned, and persuasive without being heavy-handed—advocating for the expansion as an investment in the community's future.

"You write very well," she commented when she'd finished, handing back the marked proof.

"Thank you," Ezra said, examining her corrections. "It's a skill I've worked to develop. Good observations here—I completely missed that repeated phrase."

"It's easy to do when you're close to the material," Beth said.

Their hands brushed as he took the proof, and Beth was startled by the small jolt of awareness that traveled up her arm. She withdrew her hand quickly, disconcerted.

"Indeed," Ezra agreed, seemingly unaware of her momentary discomfort. "Now, let's review tomorrow's layout."

He spread out a diagram on his desk, showing the planned arrangement of articles, announcements, and advertisements for the Wednesday edition. Beth leaned over to see better, careful to maintain a proper distance.

"We try to balance the content," Ezra explained. "Important news at the front, of course, but interspersed with community items that people care about—announcements of births, marriages, visitors to town. The middle section typically contains longer articles of general interest, while the back page is primarily advertisements."

The bell above the door jangled again, and a tall, broad-shouldered man entered, wiping his boots carefully on the doormat. He bore a distinct resemblance to Ezra—the same strong jawline and intelligent eyes, though his hair was sprinkled with gray, and lines of experience mapped his face.

"Pa," Ezra said, straightening up with evident pleasure. "What brings you to town?"

"Supply run," the older man said, his deep voice carrying easily in the small office. "Your mother wanted fabric for new curtains, and we needed grain for the horses." His gaze shifted to Beth, curious but not intrusive.

"Pa, this is Miss Elizabeth Beaumont, newly arrived from St. Louis and my new assistant at the Herald," Ezra said. "Miss Beaumont, may I present my father, Jacob Simmons."

"Pleased to meet you, sir," Beth said politely.

"Likewise, Miss Beaumont," Jacob replied, studying her with kind but perceptive eyes. "I hope my boy is treating you well."

"Very well, thank you," Beth assured him. "Mr. Simmons has been most patient in teaching me the essentials of newspaper work."

"Good to hear," Jacob said with a nod. "Ezra takes after his mother in that regard—she was a natural teacher." He turned back to his son. "Your mother wants to know when you're coming out to the ranch for dinner. Says she hardly sees you these days."

"I've been busy with the newspaper," Ezra said, a note of apology in his voice. "But things should settle now that Miss Beaumont is here to help. Perhaps Sunday, after church?"

"She'd like that," Jacob agreed. He glanced at Beth again. "You're welcome too, Miss Beaumont. My wife enjoys meeting new folks, especially from back East. She doesn't get to town as often as she'd like these days."

Beth was touched by the casual kindness of the invitation. "That's very kind, Mr. Simmons, but I wouldn't want to intrude on family time."

Jacob waved off her concern. "Nonsense. Our table always has room for one more. Besides, if you're working with Ezra, you're practically family now. The Herald is as much his child as any flesh and blood offspring."

Ezra rolled his eyes slightly at his father's comment but didn't contradict him. "We'll see how Miss Beaumont is settled by then," he said diplomatically. "It's been rather a whirlwind for her since arriving."

"Of course, of course," Jacob agreed easily. "The invitation stands whenever it suits." He checked the large pocket watch from his vest. "I should be getting back. Your mother will wonder if I've been waylaid by road agents if I'm much later." He nodded to Beth. "A pleasure meeting you, Miss Beaumont. Welcome to Hopewell Creek."

After Jacob departed, Ezra returned to explaining the layout process, but Beth found herself distracted by the simple warmth of his father's welcome and the casual assumption that she would be part of Ezra's circle now. It was a far cry from the cool assessment in Rosalind Fairfield's gaze.

As the afternoon waned and the light outside began to soften, Beth realized how physically and mentally tired she was. Her back ached from the unaccustomed posture of setting type, and her fingers were stained with ink despite her efforts to be careful.

Ezra must have noticed her fatigue because he straightened up from the layout he was finalizing and said, "I think that's enough for your first day, Miss Beaumont. You've made remarkable progress."

"Are you sure?" Beth asked, reluctant to leave work unfinished. "I thought we were printing tomorrow's edition."

"I'll handle that part," Ezra assured her. "It's complex work that takes practice, and you've absorbed enough new information for one day."

Beth nodded, relieved but also determined not to appear weak. "Very well. What time shall I arrive in the morning?"

"Eight o'clock is fine," Ezra said. He hesitated, then added, "Shall I walk you back to the boarding house? The streets of Hopewell Creek are generally safe, but..."

"That's not necessary," Beth said quickly, though touched by his concern. "It's still daylight, and the boarding house isn't far."

Ezra frowned slightly. "Nevertheless, I would be remiss in my duties as an employer and a gentleman if I allowed you to walk unescorted, especially given recent events."

The reference to Henry Dobbins was oblique but clear. Beth realized that refusing his offer might seem ungrateful or prideful. "If you insist, Mr. Simmons."

"I do," he said firmly, reaching for his hat. "And since we'll be working closely together, perhaps you might consider calling me Ezra? 'Mr. Simmons' makes me feel like my father."

The request was reasonable, Beth acknowledged, especially in the informal atmosphere of the western town. "Ezra, then," she agreed. "And you may call me Beth, if you wish."

"Beth," he repeated, as if testing the name. "It suits you—straight-forward and unpretentious."

She wasn't sure if that was a compliment, but she chose to take it as one.

They walked together through the waning afternoon light, Ezra slightly shortening his stride to match her pace. The streets were still busy with people completing their day's business before heading home for supper.

"Would it be intrusive to ask about your life in St. Louis? Ezra asked as they walked.

Beth tensed at the question, but perhaps it was better to address it directly than to have him wondering. "My parents were once good, God-fearing people," she said, choosing her words carefully. "After my brother William died—he was a soldier—they changed. Grief led them to seek solace in gambling, then drink. Our home became..." She paused, searching for a diplomatic description. "Uncomfortable. I needed to get away. I needed to chart my own course and build a life of my own."

Ezra listened without interrupting, his expression thoughtful. "I'm sorry," he said simply when she finished. "Loss affects people differ-ently, but it's particularly hard when those we rely on falter."

"Yes," Beth agreed, grateful for his understanding. "I don't blame them, not really. Grief can be a powerful force. But I couldn't stay and watch it any longer."

"I understand the need for a fresh start," Ezra said quietly. "Many people come west for similar reasons—to leave behind painful circumstances and begin anew. There's no shame in that."

His words offered a comfort Beth needed. She'd carried so much guilt about leaving her parents, despite knowing she couldn't have stayed.

"Thank you," she said simply.

They walked in companionable silence for a moment before Ezra spoke again. "I lost my younger sister to fever when I was sixteen," he said, his voice low. "Ellen was only twelve. My mother... she withdrew into herself for nearly a year afterward. Barely spoke, hardly ate. My father and I feared we might lose her, too."

Beth glanced at him, surprised by this personal revelation. "I'm sorry. That must have been terribly difficult."

"It was," Ezra acknowledged. "But eventually, she found her way back to us—and to her faith. It taught me that healing isn't always straightforward or quick, but it is possible."

"Your father mentioned your mother doesn't come to town often..." Beth asked, recalling Jacob Simmons' comment.

Ezra nodded. "She had the fever as well... it affected her lungs. She recovered, but remains susceptible to illness. She manages the household at the ranch and lives a full life, but needs to be careful about overexertion. Ever since Ellen passed, she much prefers to stay close to home."

They turned onto the quieter street where Mrs. Jenkins' boarding house stood. The late afternoon shadows were lengthening, and lamps were being lit in windows along the street.

"I should thank you," Beth said as they approached the boarding house. "Not just for employing me, but for your kindness today. It would have been easy to treat me with pity or suspicion, given the circumstances of my arrival. Instead, you've treated me with respect."

Ezra stopped at the gate to Mrs. Jenkins' yard, turning to face her. In the golden light, his features seemed softer, his hazel eyes warmer. "You deserve respect, Beth. You've shown remarkable courage and dignity in difficult circumstances. Those are qualities I admire."

The sincerity in his voice made Beth's cheeks warm. "You've known me less than two days," she reminded him, though without rancor. "I could be a terrible disappointment once you know me better."

A smile crinkled the corners of his eyes. "I don't think so. I'm a reasonably good judge of character—a necessary skill in my profession. But I suppose time will tell." He opened the gate for her. "Eight o'clock tomorrow, then?"

"I'll be there," Beth promised. "Goodnight, Ezra."

"Goodnight, Beth. Rest well."

As she climbed the steps to the boardinghouse porch, Beth glanced back. Ezra was still standing at the gate, hat in hand, watching to ensure she entered safely. The simple courtesy touched something in her that had been dormant for a long time—a sense that perhaps she mattered, that her wellbeing was of concern to someone else.

Inside, Mrs. Jenkins called from the kitchen, "Is that you, Beth? Supper's nearly ready!"

"Yes, Mrs. Jenkins. I'll just wash up." Beth headed to her room, noting the pleasant aroma of beef stew wafting through the house.

In her room, she studied her reflection in the small mirror above the washstand. Her appearance was hardly different from this morning—perhaps a bit more disheveled, with a tiny smudge of printer's ink on her chin and strands of honey-blonde hair escaping her practical knot. Yet, she felt different—more solid somehow, as if the day's work and small courtesies had begun to anchor her in this new place.

"Thank you, Lord," she whispered, the prayer coming more naturally than it had this morning. "I don't know if this is Your plan for me, but I'm grateful for this day and the kindness I've been shown."

Chapter 10

Beth arrived at the Herald office fifteen minutes before eight, determined to be punctual on her second day. The streets of Hopewell Creek were already bustling with morning activity—merchants sweeping their storefronts, wagons delivering goods, and townspeople beginning their daily routines. The air carried the scent of baking bread from the Danvers Bakery down the street, making her stomach rumble despite Mrs. Jenkins' hearty breakfast of porridge and toast.

She paused outside the newspaper office, noticing the front window was already illuminated. Ezra was clearly an early riser. Taking a deep breath, she smoothed her dress—a practical navy blue with tiny white dots—and entered.

The bell jangled as she stepped inside. Ezra emerged from behind the printing press, sleeves rolled up and hands already stained with ink. His face brightened when he saw her.

"Good morning," he said. "You're early."

"Good morning." Beth hung her shawl on the coat rack near the door. "I thought I might review yesterday's lessons before we began."

"Commendable dedication," Ezra said with approval. "Today will be busy—Wednesday is publication day. The town will soon be wanting their weekly Herald."

Beth moved to her small desk, arranging her things with care. "What shall I do first?"

"I've set most of the type for the front page already, but there are two columns on page two that need finishing. I thought you might try your hand at it while I make final adjustments to the press." He indicated a neatly written sheet of paper. "This is Sheriff Miller's notice about vagrancy laws. It needs to be set exactly as written—legal notices must be precise."

Beth studied the paper, mentally calculating the type she would need. She moved to the type cases with more confidence than yesterday, remembering the layout Ezra had taught her. The small metal letters felt more familiar in her fingers today.

"Was your evening restful?" Ezra asked as he adjusted a lever on the press.

"Yes, thank you. Mrs. Jenkins is a kind hostess. She insists on feeding me enough for three people, however." Beth selected a 'P' from its compartment.

Ezra chuckled. "She does the same with everyone. Says skinny people make her nervous."

"She mentioned you take most of your meals at the O'Leary Café."

"I do," Ezra confirmed, testing the press's roller. "My cooking skills are limited to coffee and frying bacon. The café is convenient, and the food is excellent."

Beth worked steadily, thinking of Ezra living alone, taking meals at the café. It painted a rather solitary picture. Had he never wished for a wife to share his home? She pushed the thought away, focusing on the type. It wasn't her place to wonder about such things.

The front door opened and a tall, robust woman with soft red hair pulled into a practical bun entered, carrying a basket covered with a checkered cloth.

"Morning, Ezra," she called cheerfully. "Brought you some fresh muffins for publication day. I know you'll be working through lunch."

"Mrs. O'Leary, you're a saint among women," Ezra said, setting down his tools. "This is Miss Elizabeth Beaumont, my new assistant."

Mrs. O'Leary turned keen green eyes toward Beth. "So you're the young lady everyone's talking about. Maggie mentioned meeting you yesterday." She set the basket on Ezra's desk and approached Beth, extending a work-worn hand. "Harriet O'Leary. My husband, Patrick and I run the café and general store."

Beth shook her hand, noting the firm grip. "Pleased to meet you, Mrs. O'Leary. Your daughter was very kind yesterday."

"Maggie's got a good heart," Mrs. O'Leary said proudly. "Sometimes too good—takes on more than she should." She turned to Ezra. "Which reminds me of my errand. Need to place an advertisement in today's paper. We're seeking help at the café."

Ezra reached for his notepad. "Is Maggie leaving?"

"Goodness, no," Mrs. O'Leary said, shaking her head. "But she's running herself ragged between the store and café. Patrick's getting older, his arthritis is acting up something fierce, and I can't manage both places alone. We need another pair of hands, especially during the midday rush."

"I'll make sure it's prominent," Ezra promised, jotting notes. "Any particular qualifications?"

"Someone who works hard and doesn't mind heat. Cooking experience preferred, but not necessary—I can teach anyone with sense how to follow instructions." Mrs. O'Leary cast an appraising glance at Beth. "You settling in alright, Miss Beaumont?"

"Yes, thank you," Beth replied, surprised by the direct question.

"Good. Don't let this town's gossips trouble you. Most folks here are decent, just curious about newcomers." She adjusted her shawl. "You should come by the store sometime. I got a shipment of fabrics in last week—some pretty calicos that might suit you. And you're welcome at our table anytime. First meal's on the house for newcomers."

The woman's brisk kindness touched Beth. "That's very generous."

"Not generosity, just good business," Mrs. O'Leary replied with a wink. "Feed folks well once, and they'll come back."

Ezra finished writing the advertisement details. "How does this sound? 'Help wanted: O'Leary Café seeks a hardworking assistant for a busy establishment. Cooking experience is valued, but willingness to learn is essential. Inquire within. Competitive wages offered.'"

"Perfect," Mrs. O'Leary nodded. "Add that meals are included. That's a draw for some."

"Will do." Ezra made the addition.

Mrs. O'Leary turned back to Beth. "Don't let him work you too hard. Ezra gets tunnel vision on publication days—forgets people need to eat and rest."

"I'll manage," Beth assured her, warming to the woman's motherly concern.

"She's already proving invaluable," Ezra said. "Her typesetting skills are developing remarkably quickly."

Beth felt a flush of pleasure at the compliment.

"Well, I'll leave you to it. Need to get back before the breakfast crowd thins." Mrs. O'Leary headed for the door, then paused. "Oh—nearly forgot. Pastor Paul's wife is organizing a quilting circle on Saturday afternoon at the church. It's a good way to meet the ladies of the town... I expect to see you there."

"Thank you, I'll consider it," Beth said, though the prospect of facing a room full of curious women made her stomach tighten.

After Mrs. O'Leary departed, Ezra uncovered the basket of muffins. "Would you like one? Mrs. O'Leary's blueberry muffins are renowned throughout the county."

The warm, sweet aroma was too tempting to resist. "Yes, please."

Ezra brought the basket to her desk, and Beth selected a golden-brown muffin. The first bite was heavenly—buttery, sweet, and bursting with berries.

"These are delicious," she said, savoring the flavor.

"One of the many reasons the O'Leary Café is always busy." Ezra took a muffin for himself. "Harriet O'Leary is one of Hopewell Creek's treasures. Tough as nails, but kind-hearted. She and Patrick were among the first settlers here years ago."

"She seems very... direct."

"Indeed," Ezra agreed with a smile. "Says exactly what she's thinking, which can be startling but refreshing. No games or hidden meanings with Harriet."

They returned to work, Beth focusing on setting the sheriff's notice while Ezra prepared the press. The morning passed quickly, with Beth completing the notice and moving on to setting a column of community announcements—births, marriages, and visitors to the town.

Around ten o'clock, Ezra announced it was time to begin printing. He showed Beth how to ink the rollers properly and position the paper for clean, even printing.

"The trick is consistent pressure," he explained, demonstrating the smooth pull of the press lever. "Too gentle and the ink won't transfer properly; too forceful and you'll smudge everything."

Beth watched attentively, fascinated by the mechanical precision of the process. When Ezra invited her to try, she approached the press with determination.

Her first attempt produced a slightly uneven impression, but her second was cleaner. By the fifth sheet, she had developed a steady rhythm.

"Excellent," Ezra said, inspecting the freshly printed page. "You have a natural feel for it."

His approval warmed her more than it should have.

They worked side by side, printing the first batch of papers. Beth was surprised by how physically demanding the process was—her arms ached from pulling the press lever, and her back protested from standing in one position for so long. Yet, there was satisfaction in seeing the blank pages transform into neatly printed newspapers.

"We'll take a short break while this ink sets," Ezra said eventually. "Then we'll print the reverse sides."

Beth gratefully straightened, pressing a hand against the small of her back.

"Sore?" Ezra asked, noticing her discomfort.

"A little," she admitted. "I'm not accustomed to standing so long in one position."

"The first few weeks are the hardest," Ezra said sympathetically. "My back and shoulders were in constant revolt when I first started. But your body adjusts."

Beth moved to the window, stretching discreetly. Outside, the town was fully awake now, with people moving purposefully along the boardwalks and wagons rattling down the street.

"It's remarkable how quickly a town comes together each morning," she observed. "Like a complex mechanism with each person playing their part."

Ezra joined her at the window. "An apt comparison. I've often thought the same." He stood close enough that Beth could detect the faint scent of soap and ink that seemed to define him. "Everyone has their role—merchant, blacksmith, teacher, lawman. Remove one piece and the mechanism falters."

"And what's the newspaper's role?" Beth asked, genuinely curious.

Ezra considered this. "Communication—the nervous system of the town, if you will. We transmit information, connect people to events and ideas they might otherwise miss." He smiled. "And occasionally, we're the conscience, pointing out what needs repair or attention."

"An important responsibility," Beth mused.

"Yes, which is why accuracy and fairness matter so much." Ezra's expression grew serious. "Words have power. They can enlighten or mislead, heal or wound."

The depth of his commitment impressed Beth. She'd never considered newspaper work as a calling, but Ezra clearly saw it that way.

Their break ended too quickly, and they returned to the press to print the reverse sides of the pages. This required careful alignment to ensure the text appeared properly on both sides. Beth found this challenging at first, but under Ezra's patient guidance, she soon developed the needed precision.

By noon, they had printed three hundred copies of the four-page Hopewell Creek Herald. The next task was folding and preparing them for distribution. They worked at Ezra's desk, creating neat stacks of folded papers.

"How do people receive their newspapers?" Beth asked, smoothing a crease.

"Various ways," Ezra explained. "Businesses and regular subscribers pay for delivery—Tom Bellwether's boy Jimmy handles that after school. Others purchase directly from the office or at the general store.

Farmers and ranchers typically pick up their copies when they come to town for supplies."

The bell jangled, and a middle-aged man with spectacles entered, his clothes dusty from travel.

"Alfred," Ezra greeted him. "Right on time."

"Always am," the man replied, removing his hat. "Got the Gazette and the Post this week." He noticed Beth and nodded politely. "Ma'am."

"Alfred brings newspapers from Denver and Colorado Springs," Ezra explained to Beth. "We exchange copies—it helps us all stay informed about regional news." He made introductions. "Alfred Jenkins, this is Miss Elizabeth Beaumont, my new assistant."

"Jenkins?" Beth repeated. "Any relation to Mrs. Jenkins of the boardinghouse?"

"My cousin," Alfred confirmed with a smile. "Clair mentioned she had a new boarder. Said you were from St. Louis."

"Yes," Beth said, suddenly self-conscious under his curious gaze.

Alfred turned his attention back to Ezra. "Herald ready?"

"Just finishing up." Ezra handed him several copies.

Alfred tucked the papers into his satchel and produced two different newspapers in exchange. "Denver's talking about railroad expansion again. Post has a lengthy article about proposed routes."

"Interesting," Ezra said, examining the papers. "Any mention of lines through our region?"

"Not specifically, but worth following. Could mean changes for towns like ours."

They chatted briefly about news from other communities before Alfred departed for the next town on his circuit.

"Alfred carries newspapers between twelve towns," Ezra explained after he'd gone. "Works for the stage company as a messenger, but does this newspaper exchange on the side. It's an informal network that serves us all well."

Beth considered the broader implications. "So you're not just reporting on Hopewell Creek—you're connecting it to the wider world."

"Exactly," Ezra said, pleased by her understanding. "Isolation is the enemy of progress and knowledge. Even small towns need to know what's happening beyond their borders."

They resumed folding papers, working in companionable silence for a while. Beth found herself stealing glances at Ezra's profile as he concentrated on his task. There was something appealing about the quiet intensity with which he approached his work—a steadiness that spoke of reliability and purpose.

The bell jangled again, this time announcing Sheriff Jonas Miller, a lean man with a weathered face and alert eyes beneath his broad-brimmed hat.

"Afternoon, Ezra," he said, then nodded to Beth. "Miss."

"Sheriff Miller, meet Miss Elizabeth Beaumont, my new assistant," Ezra said, rising from his chair. "Beth, this is Sheriff Jonas Miller, keeper of the peace in Hopewell Creek."

"Pleasure, Miss Beaumont," the sheriff said, studying her with frank curiosity. "Settling in alright?"

"Yes, thank you," Beth replied, beginning to feel like a curiosity on display with each new introduction.

"Good, good." He turned to Ezra. "Paper ready? Is my notice in there about the vagrancy ordinance?"

"Front page of the second section," Ezra confirmed, handing him a copy. "Beth set the type herself."

The sheriff glanced at Beth with newfound respect. "That so? Nice work, Miss Beaumont." He scanned the notice critically. "Looks correct. We're enforcing this more strictly now."

Beth sensed a story behind the increased enforcement but didn't feel it was her place to inquire.

The sheriff must have noticed her curiosity because he explained, "Had some trouble with drifters last month. Nothing serious, but better to be clear about expectations. Hopewell Creek welcomes honest folks looking for work or a fresh start, but not those aiming to make mischief."

Beth wondered if she would have been considered a vagrant if Ezra hadn't offered her employment so promptly. The thought was unsettling.

"Any other news the Herald should know about?" Ezra asked, taking a seat behind his desk.

"Nothing official," the sheriff said, leaning against the door frame. "Though there's talk the mining company might be expanding operations near Winsome Valley. Could mean more business for Hopewell Creek if it happens."

"I'll keep an ear open," Ezra promised. "Let me know if anything develops."

After the sheriff departed, more visitors began arriving—merchants and townspeople eager for the fresh edition. Ezra handled most transactions while Beth continued preparing bundles for delivery. She listened as he chatted easily with each person, answering questions about articles or taking notes for future stories.

She observed how differently people reacted to her presence. Some merely nodded politely; others openly stared; a few made pointed efforts to introduce themselves. Mrs. Turner, the milliner, examined Beth with particular attention, asking pointed questions about her background that Beth answered as honestly as possible without revealing too much about her parents' decline.

"St. Louis is quite civilized compared to our little town," Mrs. Turner said with a sniff. "You must find Hopewell Creek terribly primitive."

"Not at all," Beth replied honestly. "I find it refreshing. There's a directness here that's appealing."

Mrs. Turner seemed surprised by this response. "Well, if you need any help adjusting, I'm sure Miss Fairfield would be happy to introduce you to proper society here. Her father is our leading citizen, you know."

The mention of Rosalind Fairfield made Beth's stomach tighten, but she kept her expression neutral. "How kind."

After Mrs. Turner left, Ezra caught Beth's eye with a knowing look. "Don't let Mrs. Turner concern you. She considers herself the arbiter of social standing in Hopewell Creek, but most people pay her little mind."

"I wasn't concerned," Beth assured him, though she had been, slightly.

"Good." Ezra sorted through a stack of subscription notices. "By the way, I took the liberty of including a brief article about mail-order bride schemes. I mentioned no names, but emphasized the importance of verifying arrangements before traveling. I hope that meets with your approval."

Beth appreciated his consideration. "Yes, thank you. If it prevents another woman from experiencing what I did, it's worthwhile."

By mid-afternoon. Beth's back ached from standing, and her fingers were stained with ink despite her efforts to be careful. Yet, she felt a deep satisfaction in the day's accomplishments. She had contributed meaningfully to creating something that would inform and connect the community.

"I think we've earned a proper lunch," Ezra declared, hanging the "Back in 60 Minutes," sign on the door. "Would you join me at the O'Leary Café? Mrs. O'Leary's invitation this morning reminded me I haven't properly welcomed you to Hopewell Creek with a proper meal."

Beth hesitated, uncertain if accepting would be proper. "I wouldn't want to impose."

"It's not an imposition—it's lunch," Ezra said with a smile that softened his features. "Besides, you should experience Mrs. O'Leary's cooking properly, not just her muffins or a simple sandwich."

"Very well," Beth agreed, untying her ink-stained apron. She glanced down at her dress, noticing a small spot of ink on the sleeve. "Though I'm hardly presentable."

"Everyone in town knows it's publication day," Ezra said, rolling down his sleeves and donning his vest. "A bit of printer's ink is expected."

They stepped out into the bright afternoon. The air was crisp and clear, carrying the scent of pine from the distant mountains. Beth took a deep breath, savoring the freshness after hours in the ink-scented office.

Chapter 11

The O'Leary Café was just two doors down from the Herald office—a cheerful establishment with gingham curtains in the windows and a hand-painted sign out front. When they entered, the savory aromas of roasting meat and baked bread enveloped them. The café was busy but not crowded, with most tables occupied by locals enjoying late lunches.

Maggie O'Leary spotted them immediately and waved them to a small table near the front window. "Newspaper day," she said with a grin. "Mama's Irish stew is today's special, fresh bread and apple for dessert."

"Sounds perfect," Ezra said, holding Beth's chair for her. "We're famished."

"I'll bring water right away," Maggie promised, hurrying off.

Beth glanced around the café, taking in the simple, homey atmosphere. Checkered cloths covered the tables, and curtains of the same pattern framed the windows. The walls were decorated with landscape paintings and a few old photographs of early Hopewell Creek.

"This is lovely," she said, appreciating the warmth and comfortable atmosphere.

"One of Hopewell Creek's institutions," Ezra agreed. "The O'Leary's started with just a small general store. The café came later when Mrs. O'Leary's reputation for good cooking spread. Now they run both, with Maggie helping at each as needed."

Maggie returned with water and two large bowls of fragrant stew accompanied by thick slices of crusty bread. "Mama says this meal's on the house."

"Oh, but—" Beth began to protest.

"No arguing with Mama," Maggie said firmly. "It's a tradition for newcomers. Mr. Simmons can pay for his own, though." She winked at Ezra, who laughed good-naturedly.

"Your mother mentioned needing help," Beth said. "Is business that busy?"

"Especially at midday and evenings," Maggie confirmed. "I used to manage fine splitting time between here and the store, but since Hannah Whitaker married and moved to Denver last week, we've been short-handed. It can't be in two places at once." She glanced around to ensure no customers required attention. "How's your first few days at the Herald?"

"Educational," Beth replied with a smile. "I've learned more about printing in two days than I knew existed."

"She's a natural," Ezra added, breaking off a piece of bread. "Already setting type and operating the press."

Maggie looked impressed. "Fast learner, then. That'll serve you well here. Hopewell Creek may be small, but we move at a quick pace."

After Maggie left to attend to other customers, Beth sampled the stew. It was delicious—rich with tender beef, vegetables, and herbs she couldn't identify, but that melded perfectly.

"This is wonderful," she said, savoring another spoonful.

"Mrs. O'Leary could have opened a fine restaurant in Denver," Ezra said. "Fortunately for us, she prefers Hopewell Creek's simpler pace."

Beth enjoyed the normalcy of the moment—sharing a meal in a pleasant café, the hubbub of conversation around them, sunlight filtering through the gingham curtains. It felt ordinary in the best possible way, a respite from the uncertainty and tension of recent days.

"May I ask you something?" she ventured after a while.

"Of course."

"Why did you decide to become a newspaper editor? Was it a family business?"

Ezra set down his spoon, considering the question. "No, though my father always encouraged reading and staying informed. My grandfather was actually a teacher, and I originally thought I might follow that path." He broke off another piece of bread. "I attended two years of college in Denver—studied literature and history. But during breaks, I worked for The Denver Post, first just sweeping floors and running errands, then gradually learning to typeset and writing."

"You discovered a passion for it," Beth surmised.

"Yes. I found I loved the immediate impact of journalism—how today's news becomes tomorrow's history. When I heard Hopewell Creek's former newspaper owner wanted to retire and move east, I saw an opportunity." His expression grew reflective. "I was twenty-three, probably overconfident, but my father helped with the initial investment, and here I am, five years later."

"You've never regretted returning to a small town after experiencing Denver?"

"Never," Ezra said firmly. "Denver has its attractions, certainly, but there's something deeply satisfying about serving a community where you know every reader personally. Where you can see the direct impact of your work." He tilted his head, studying her. "What about you? Did you have aspirations before circumstances led you here?"

Beth considered this. No one had asked about her dreams in a very long time. "I enjoyed learning," she said slowly. "I had a good teacher in elementary school who encouraged my interest in literature. For a while, I thought I might become a teacher myself someday."

"That's still possible," Ezra pointed out.

Beth smiled sadly. "Perhaps. But after my brother died and my parents... changed, education became secondary to managing day-to-day life."

"I understand," Ezra said quietly. "Necessity often redirects our paths."

The conversation paused as Maggie brought apple pie—golden-crusted and fragrant with cinnamon.

"Mama's specialty," she announced proudly. "Extra cinnamon, just how Mr. Simmons likes it."

"Mrs. O'Leary spoils me," Ezra admitted after Maggie departed.

"It seems you're well-looked after in Hopewell Creek," Beth observed, taking a bite of the pie. The perfect balance of tart apples and sweet, spiced filling nearly made her close her eyes in appreciation.

"I'm fortunate in my friends," Ezra agreed. "Though they're not subtle about certain matters."

"What do you mean?"

Ezra looked slightly embarrassed. "Let's just say Mrs. O'Leary, like several other ladies in town, has rather transparent hopes regarding my marital status."

Beth felt her cheeks warm. "Ah. Mrs. Jenkins mentioned something similar."

"I suspected as much." Ezra shook his head ruefully. "Small towns have their disadvantages—privacy being chief among them. Everyone knows your business and feels entitled to an opinion on it."

"It comes from caring, I suppose," Beth suggested.

"Mostly, yes. Though sometimes mere curiosity." He changed the subject smoothly. "Have you thought about Mrs. O'Leary's invitation to visit the quilting circle on Saturday?"

"I'm not sure," Beth admitted.

"You're concerned about facing all the town ladies at once," Ezra finished perceptively.

"Yes," Beth acknowledged. "Their curiosity is understandable, but I'd rather not be the center of attention."

"Mary Hawthorne—the pastor's wife—is a kind woman who won't allow anyone to make you uncomfortable," Ezra assured her. "And it would be a good opportunity to establish yourself independent of... the circumstances of your arrival."

He had a point. Avoiding social gatherings would only fuel gossip and speculation. "I'll consider it," she promised.

They finished their meal, and Ezra insisted on paying, despite Maggie's assurance that Beth's portion was complimentary. As they were preparing to leave, Mrs. O'Leary emerged from the kitchen, wiping her hands on her apron.

"Well? How'd you like your first O'Leary meal?" she asked Beth directly.

"It was wonderful," Beth said sincerely. "I've never tasted such delicious stew or pie."

Mrs. O'Leary beamed. "Good. You're welcome anytime." She glanced at Ezra. "This one knows he's always got a place at our table."

"And I'm grateful for it," Ezra said. "Your cooking keeps this town functioning, Mrs. O'Leary."

The woman chuckled. "Flattery might get you an extra slice of pie next time, Ezra Simmons." She turned to Beth. "Hope you'll consider coming to the quilting circle on Saturday. Mary specifically mentioned, hoping you'd join. We're working on a wedding quilt for the Peterson girl."

"I'll be there," Beth found herself saying, unable to refuse the woman's direct invitation.

"Good." Mrs. O'Leary nodded with satisfaction. "Two o'clock at the church. Bring a thimble if you have one. Don't worry if you're not an expert with a needle—plenty aren't. It's really just an excuse for conversation, anyway."

Back at the newspaper office, they found several customers waiting in line outside the door for copies of the Herald. The afternoon passed quickly as they handled sales, prepared mail subscriptions, and began planning the next edition.

"Typically, I use Thursdays for gathering news and writing," Ezra explained as they organized the desk. "Fridays for planning the layout and beginning typesetting. Monday and Tuesday for completing typesetting and making corrections. Wednesday for printing and distribution. Then the cycle begins again."

"A continuous process," Beth noted.

"Exactly. The news doesn't stop, so neither do we." He glanced at the wall clock. "It's nearly five. I think we can consider today a success."

Beth looked around at the now-orderly office, feeling a sense of accomplishment. "It's satisfying, seeing the physical results of our work."

"One of the best parts of this profession," Ezra agreed. "Tangible evidence of effort." He hesitated, then added, "I realize you might be tired, but if you're amenable, I thought we might take a brief tour of

Hopewell Creek before returning to Mrs. Jenkins. You've seen little beyond the Herald office and boarding house."

The idea appealed to Beth. "I'd like that."

They secured the office, and Ezra guided Beth along Main Street, pointing out significant buildings and businesses. The town was larger than Beth had initially realized, with several cross streets branching from the main thoroughfare.

"That's the schoolhouse." Ezra indicated a white clapboard building setback from the street, with a small bell tower atop its roof. "Miss Agnes Preston teaches all eight grades—about thirty children currently. She's been here almost as long as the O'Leary's."

They passed Bellwether's Blacksmith Shop, where the rhythmic clang of hammer on anvil rang out, then the livery stable operated by the Crawford brothers. Ezra nodded to people they encountered, making introductions when appropriate.

"The Fairfield Bank," he said as they approached an imposing brick building with large windows. "The only brick structure in town currently, a point of pride for Walter Fairfield."

The bank doors opened, and Rosalind Fairfield emerged, accompanied by an older man with the same proud bearing and aristocratic features.

"Ezra," Rosalind called, her face lighting up. "How fortunate to encounter you." Her gaze flickered to Beth, the warmth in her expression cooling noticeably.

"Miss Fairfield," Ezra replied politely. "Mr. Fairfield. Allow me to introduce Miss Elizabeth Beaumont, my new assistant at the Herald."

Walter Fairfield assessed Beth with calculating eyes. He was a distinguished man of perhaps sixty, with silver hair and an immaculate suit that spoke of wealth, unusual for a frontier town.

"Miss Beaumont," he said with a slight nod. "I understand you've recently arrived from St. Louis."

"Yes, sir," Beth replied, maintaining what she hoped was a composed demeanor.

"A significant change, I imagine. St. Louis is considerably more... established than our humble community."

"Different, certainly," Beth agreed. "But Hopewell Creek has its own distinct character and charm."

"Indeed," Mr. Fairfield said, his tone suggesting he found her response diplomatic rather than sincere. "Well, we welcome newcomers, particularly those with... useful skills." He turned to Ezra. "The latest edition of the Herald arrived at the bank. I noticed your article about railroad expansion possibilities. Interesting speculation."

"Merely reporting what's being discussed in Denver, with more to come next week," Ezra said. "If you have insights about potential economic impacts for Hopewell Creek, I'd value your perspective for a follow-up piece."

"Perhaps. Stop by the bank tomorrow afternoon if you wish to discuss it." Mr. Fairfield checked his pocket watch. "Rosalind, we should continue. Your mother expects us for dinner at six."

"Of course, Father." Rosalind smiled at Ezra. "The Literary Society meets tomorrow evening at our home. I do hope you'll attend, Ezra. We're discussing Emerson's essays."

"Thank you for the reminder," Ezra said. "I'll try to be there if my schedule permits."

"You're welcome too, Miss Beaumont," Rosalind added, though her tone lacked enthusiasm. "If you enjoy literature."

"That's very kind," Beth said, uncertain if the invitation was sincere or merely proper form.

"Until tomorrow, perhaps," Rosalind said to Ezra, then departed with her father.

They continued their walk, passing a law office, a small dressmaker's shop, and finally reaching the church at the end of the main street.

"The town originally grew around the church," Ezra explained. "Pastor Paul's father was the first minister here, when Hopewell Creek was just a cluster of cabins."

The white church with its simple steeple looked peaceful in the late afternoon light. Beth felt drawn to its quiet dignity.

"Would you like to look inside?" Ezra asked, noticing her interest.

"I visited briefly the day I arrived. Is it open?"

"Always. Pastor Paul believes God's house should never be locked to those seeking solace."

They climbed the few steps to the church door, which opened silently on well-oiled hinges. The interior was cool and dim, with sunlight filtering through simple stained-glass windows, casting colored patterns on the wooden pews. The smell of beeswax and aged wood created an atmosphere of reverence.

Beth moved slowly down the center aisle, admiring the craftsmanship of the altar and pulpit. It was a modest church by big-city standards, but there was genuine beauty in its simplicity and evident care.

She stopped before the altar, where a large wooden cross hung on the wall. For the first time in days, Beth felt a stirring of the faith—a quiet reassurance that perhaps God hadn't forgotten her after all.

"This church is so beautiful," she said softly.

"Yes," Ezra agreed, his voice equally quiet in the sacred space. "Not grand, but sincere—built by the hands and hearts of people who believed in something greater than themselves."

They stood in companionable silence for a moment. Beth whispered a prayer of gratitude for the unexpected kindness she'd found in Hopewell Creek.

The church door opened behind them, and Pastor Paul entered, looking surprised but pleased to find them there.

"Ezra, Miss Beaumont," he greeted them warmly. "What a pleasant surprise."

"I was showing Beth around town," Ezra explained. "We hope we're not intruding."

"Not at all," the pastor assured them. "God's house welcomes all, especially those seeking to know the community better." He smiled at Beth. "How are you settling in, Miss Beaumont?"

"Well, thank you," Beth replied. "Everyone has been very kind."

"I'm glad to hear it. Mary mentioned she hopes to see you at the quilting circle. I hope you'll join them."

"I'm planning to," Beth confirmed. "Mrs. O'Leary was quite persuasive."

Pastor Paul chuckled. "Harriet O'Leary has a way of offering suggestions that feel like divine commandments. But you'll enjoy the circle—it's a wonderful way to become acquainted with the heart of our community." He glanced at the windows, where the light was beginning to take on the golden quality of late afternoon. "Will you be joining us for Sunday services?"

"Yes," Beth said without hesitation, surprising herself with the certainty in her voice. "I'd like that very much."

"Excellent. Our service begins at ten. Nothing elaborate, but we worship with sincere hearts." He turned to Ezra. "And you, Ezra? We've missed you these past few Sundays."

Ezra looked slightly abashed. "The Herald has kept me busy, but I'll be there this week. I promised my mother, in any case."

"Good man," Pastor Paul said with approval. "I'll leave you to your tour. I just came to retrieve my Bible for this evening's study group." He moved toward the pulpit.

As they stepped outside, the church bell rang once—a single, clear tone that seemed to hang in the air before fading.

"Five o'clock," Ezra explained. "The bell rings at noon and five each day. A tradition from when fewer people owned timepieces."

They descended the church steps and began walking back toward Main Street. The angle of the sun had changed, casting longer shadows and bathing the buildings in warm, golden light.

"What else would you like to see?" Ezra asked.

Beth considered this. "Perhaps the creek itself? I've arrived in a town named Hopewell Creek, but haven't yet laid eyes on it."

Ezra smiled. "An excellent suggestion. It's not far—just beyond the eastern edge of town."

They walked past the schoolhouse again and followed a well-worn path that led away from the buildings. After a few minutes, Beth heard the gentle sound of flowing water.

The creek appeared before them—a clear, bubbling stream winding its way through a small meadow dotted with wildflowers. Cottonwood trees lined its banks, their leaves rustling in the afternoon breeze. The water caught the sunlight, sparkling like scattered diamonds.

"It's lovely," Beth breathed, enchanted by the peaceful scene.

"The town's lifeblood," Ezra said. "Never runs dry, even in the driest summers. The early settlers saw it as a sign of God's provision—a place where hope wells up continuously. Hence, Hopewell Creek."

They found a smooth boulder near the water's edge and sat down, watching the creek's steady flow. A pair of birds darted over the surface, catching insects in mid-flight.

"Do you think you could be content here?" Ezra asked after a comfortable silence. "In Hopewell Creek, I mean. It's very different from St. Louis."

Beth considered the question seriously. "I believe I could," she said finally. "There's a... genuineness here that I find appealing. In St. Louis, especially in recent years, I often felt I was playing a part—pretending our family was still what it had once been, hiding the truth of our circumstances." She trailed her fingers in the cool water. "Here, despite being a stranger, I feel less need for pretense."

"Small towns can be judgmental," Ezra cautioned. "But they can also be extraordinarily forgiving and supportive when someone is honest about their struggles."

"Like you've been, with my situation," Beth said quietly.

"I've merely offered what anyone would," Ezra demurred.

"No," Beth shook her head. "Not anyone. Many would have turned away, especially knowing I arrived as a mail-order bride. You saw a person in need, not just a situation to avoid."

Ezra looked slightly uncomfortable with her praise. "Perhaps I recognized something of myself in your determination. We all need someone to believe in us at critical moments."

A comfortable silence fell between them, filled only by the gentle murmur of the creek and distant birdsong. Beth felt a curious sense of peace—the first true calm she'd experienced since leaving St. Louis. Whatever lay ahead, she no longer felt adrift.

"We should head back," Ezra said eventually, noting the lengthening shadows. "Mrs. Jenkins will worry if you're late for dinner."

They rose and followed the path back toward town. The air was growing cooler with the approaching evening, and Beth wrapped her shawl more tightly around her shoulders.

"Thank you for the tour," she said as the buildings of Hopewell Creek came back into view. "And for lunch. It was kind of you to take so much time."

"It was my pleasure," Ezra replied sincerely. "Having lived here most of my life, I sometimes forget to appreciate what makes Hopewell Creek special. Seeing it through your eyes today was... refreshing."

When they reached Mrs. Jenkins' boarding house, Ezra stopped at the gate.

"I'll see you at the office tomorrow morning," he said. "We'll begin planning next week's edition."

"I look forward to it," Beth replied, and realized she truly did.

As she climbed the porch steps, Beth turned back once. Ezra still stood at the gate, waiting to ensure she entered safely. He raised his hand in a small wave, which she returned before stepping inside.

Chapter 12

"Good morning," Beth called, hanging her shawl on the coat rack after entering the Herald office the next morning.

Ezra emerged from behind the printing press, shirtsleeves rolled to his elbows and a smudge of ink on his forearm. "Morning. You're quite early today," he said, genuine pleasure in his voice.

"I thought I might get a head start on organizing." She gestured to the stack of papers on her desk. "I see you began your day early as well."

"Couldn't sleep," he admitted. "Had an idea for the railroad article that wouldn't leave me be. Thought I might as well put it to paper."

Beth noticed the coffee pot steaming on the small stove in the corner. "May I?" she asked, gesturing toward it.

"Please. Help yourself."

She poured herself a cup, appreciating the rich aroma. "Would you like one as well?"

"Already working on my second," he said, pointing to a half-empty mug beside the typesetting tray. "Hazard of early morning inspiration—it requires fuel."

Beth smiled and moved to her desk, sipping the strong black coffee as she settled in. The office was alive with morning light filtering through the large front windows, illuminating dust motes dancing in the air and the organized chaos of newspaper production.

"Mr. Simmons—"

"Ezra," he corrected gently. "If we're to work closely together, formality seems unnecessary."

She nodded. "Ezra. What would you like me to focus on today?"

He wiped his hands on a cloth and moved to his desk, retrieving a leather-bound notebook. "Thursdays are for gathering news and beginning drafts for next week's edition. I usually make rounds through town—checking with businesses, the church, local government. People expect to see the editor out collecting stories."

"And you'd like me to accompany you?" Beth asked.

"Actually, I was thinking we might divide-and-conquer today," Ezra replied. "You've met several townspeople now. Perhaps you could visit the general store, the café, and possibly the church? Pastor Paul typically has community announcements. Meanwhile, I'll handle the bank, law office, and outlying farms where I need to ride."

Beth felt a flutter of nervousness. "You trust me to gather news on my own?"

Ezra looked up, his expression sincere. "You're observant, articulate, and people seem to respond well to you. Why wouldn't I trust you?"

His confidence was both flattering and daunting. "I'll do my best," she promised.

"I have no doubt." He handed her the notebook. "Jot down anything of interest—births, deaths, visitors, business changes, upcoming events. Don't worry about crafting perfect prose yet—just gather information. We'll shape it into articles later."

They spent the next hour mapping out a plan for the upcoming edition. Beth marveled at Ezra's organized approach—he seemed to hold the entire newspaper's structure in his mind, knowing exactly how stories would fit together weeks in advance.

"The Herald prints every Wednesday," he explained, sketching a rough layout. "We need local news, some national items I get from exchange papers, advertisements, and at least one substantive article—like the railroad piece." He glanced at Beth. "I'm working on a series about potential economic developments for Hopewell Creek. The railroad expansion could bring significant changes."

"And Mr. Fairfield might help with that?" Beth asked, remembering yesterday's encounter.

Ezra nodded. "Walter Fairfield has strong opinions about development. As the town's banker, he stands to benefit from growth, but he's also protective of his influence. I try to present balanced perspectives."

Beth considered this. "Is that difficult in a small town? Being impartial when you know everyone personally?"

"One of the greatest challenges of local journalism," Ezra acknowledged. "Especially when friends or prominent citizens pressure you to slant coverage their way." He straightened papers on his desk. "But a newspaper's duty is to truth, not popularity."

"That requires courage," Beth observed.

"And occasionally thick skin," Ezra added with a wry smile. "Not everyone appreciates honest reporting when it conflicts with their interests."

The door opening interrupted their conversation. Tom Bellwether entered, carrying a small package.

"Morning, Ezra. Good morning, Miss," He nodded to them both, his large frame seeming to fill the modest office space. "Brought those replacement parts for your press. Forged them myself after studying the broken ones."

"Tom, you're a miracle worker," Ezra said, accepting the package gratefully. "Denver quoted six weeks for delivery. How much do I owe you?"

The blacksmith waved dismissively. "Consider it payment for that article you wrote about my new horseshoe design. Orders have doubled since."

"That's just good reporting, not a favor," Ezra protested.

"Then call it community support for our local paper," Tom insisted. "Besides, gives me satisfaction knowing the Herald won't miss an edition because of a broken part." He turned to Beth. "You must be Miss Beaumont. How are you finding our little town?"

"Increasingly welcoming," Beth replied sincerely. "And please, call me Beth."

Tom smiled, his weather-beaten face crinkling at the eyes. "Good to hear. Small towns can be standoffish with newcomers until they prove themselves. But you working at the Herald—that speaks well for you. Ezra doesn't suffer fools."

Beth glanced at Ezra, who looked slightly embarrassed. "I've been fortunate in the welcome I've received," she said diplomatically.

"Well, I should get back. Mrs. Crawford's mare is due for new shoes this morning." Tom headed toward the door, then paused. "Almost forgot—there's talk of the Mason family's oldest boy coming home from medical school in Chicago. Might be worth a mention in the paper. Folks are right proud of him being the first doctor born and raised in Hopewell Creek."

"When's he due back?" Ezra asked, jotting a note.

"Next month sometime. His mother mentioned it at the church social last week."

After Tom departed, Ezra turned to Beth. "That's exactly how news gathering works here. Casual mentions and overheard conversations. The challenge is sifting meaningful information from idle gossip."

"I imagine that becomes easier with experience," Beth suggested.

"And with knowing the community," Ezra agreed. "Which is why today's rounds will be valuable to you."

By mid-morning, they were ready to begin their separate news-gathering tasks. Ezra provided Beth with more specific guidance before heading out to saddle his horse for visits to outlying farms.

"We'll meet back here around noon to compare notes," he said, reaching for his hat. "Feel free to mention you're collecting items for the Herald. Most people are eager to have their announcements included."

Left alone in the office, Beth took a moment to gather her courage. This assignment represented Ezra's trust in her abilities. She straightened her dress, tucked the notebook into her pocket, and stepped out onto Main Street with newfound purpose.

The general store seemed the logical first stop. When Beth entered, scents of coffee beans, leather, spices, and soap—enveloped her. Mr. O'Leary was helping an elderly woman select fabric, while Maggie stocked shelves near the back.

"Well, look who's out and about!" Maggie exclaimed, spotting Beth. "Papa, it's Miss Beaumont from the newspaper."

Mr. O'Leary glanced up. "Ah, the new assistant editor. Harriet mentioned you enjoyed her stew yesterday."

"Very much," Beth confirmed. "Actually, I'm collecting information for next week's Herald. Ezra—Mr. Simmons—suggested your store might be a good source for community news."

"He's right about that," Maggie said, abandoning her shelving to join Beth. "Everyone passes through here, eventually. What sort of news are you after?"

"Anything of interest to the community—events, announcements, visitors."

Mr. O'Leary finished with his customer before joining the conversation. "Well, let me think. The Ladies' Aid Society is organizing a box social for the end of the month—raising funds for new hymnals. And the mercantile in Denver finally shipped those sewing machines I ordered. Three fine Singers that stitch smooth as butter. Might be worth mentioning, as several ladies have been waiting on them."

Beth dutifully noted these items, asking follow-up questions about dates and details.

Maggie leaned closer, lowering her voice conspiratorially. "If you're looking for real news, Agnes Preston at the school is apparently receiving regular letters from a gentleman in Denver. Very mysterious, as she's never mentioned a beau before."

"Maggie," her father warned, "that's speculation, not news."

"It's certainly the talk of my Tuesday sewing circle," Maggie countered.

Beth smiled diplomatically. "Perhaps I'll focus on the confirmed events for now."

After gathering several more legitimate items from the O'Leary's, Beth continued to the café, where Mrs. O'Leary proudly announced an upcoming pie contest at the summer festival. The dressmaker's shop yielded news of the latest Denver fashions arriving by mail order, and the town's small hardware store reported receiving improved kerosene lamps that burned cleaner and brighter.

Each interaction became easier than the last. Beth found that mentioning the Herald immediately opened doors and inspired people to share information. By the time she reached the church, her notebook contained a substantial collection of community happenings.

She found Pastor Paul in his small office adjacent to the sanctuary, sorting through papers.

"Miss Beaumont," he greeted her warmly. "What a pleasant surprise."

"I hope I'm not interrupting," Beth said. "I'm collecting announcements for the Herald."

"Not interrupting at all. Please, sit down." He cleared a chair of books. "I was just organizing my thoughts for Sunday's sermon." He smiled. "So Ezra has you gathering news already? He must be impressed with your capabilities."

"He's been very encouraging," Beth acknowledged, settling into the offered chair. "Do you have any church events the community should know about?"

"Indeed, we do." Pastor Paul consulted a calendar on his desk. "The Bible study group is beginning a new series on the Psalms next Thursday evening. The church picnic is scheduled for two weeks from Sunday, weather permitting. And—" he lowered his voice slightly, "—this isn't officially announced yet, but the church board has approved funds to repair the bell tower. The framework has been showing its age."

Beth recorded these items, then asked, "Is there anything else the community might find important to know?"

Pastor Paul thought for a moment. "Let's see, the quilting circle is working on Sadie Peterson's wedding quilt. They always do beautiful work. Perhaps worth noting as an example of community craftsmanship?"

"That sounds perfect for the local items section," Beth agreed, making another note.

Beth's next stop was the schoolhouse, where she found Miss Preston supervising children during their mid-morning recess. The teacher, a composed woman with intelligent eyes and a practical manner, seemed pleased by Beth's introduction.

"The Herald is an essential institution," Miss Preston said as they watched children playing in the schoolyard. "Especially for education. Several of my older students read it regularly for current events discussions."

"That's wonderful to hear," Beth replied. "Do you have any school news to share?"

"As a matter of fact, yes. The children are preparing a recitation program for the end of term—poetry, historical speeches, and musical performances. Parents and community members are welcome to attend. And—" she brightened, "—I've just received confirmation that my request for additional science materials has been approved by the school board. New botanical specimens and a proper microscope will arrive next month."

Miss Preston's enthusiasm for education impressed Beth. "You seem very dedicated to your students."

"Teaching is not merely a profession to me, but a calling," Miss Preston replied. "These children represent our community's future. They deserve the finest education we can provide, even in a frontier setting."

Beth nodded. "I was fortunate to have a teacher who inspired my love of learning. Her influence remained long after my formal education ended."

"The best teachers leave such legacies," Miss Preston agreed. "I hope to do the same."

By noon, Beth's notebook was filled with community news. She returned to the Herald office, invigorated by her morning's work and the connections she'd begun to form. The office was still empty—Ezra hadn't yet returned from his rounds to the outlying farms.

Beth took the opportunity to organize her notes, separating announcements by type and importance. She was so absorbed in the task that she didn't hear the door open until a shadow fell across her desk.

"Working hard, I see."

Beth looked up, startled to find Rosalind Fairfield standing before her desk. The banker's daughter was impeccably dressed in a fashionable blue walking suit that emphasized her slender figure, her golden hair arranged in a sophisticated style beneath a small, elegant hat.

"Miss Fairfield," Beth acknowledged, rising from her seat. "Good afternoon."

"I was hoping to find Ezra," Rosalind said, glancing around the empty office.

"He's gathering news from the farms outside town," Beth explained. "He should return soon if you'd like to wait."

Rosalind considered this, then gracefully settled into the chair beside Beth's desk. "I suppose I can spare a few minutes." Her gaze swept over Beth's neat stack of notes. "Collecting local gossip for the paper?"

Something in her tone made Beth bristle slightly, but she maintained a pleasant expression. "Community news items, yes. There's quite a lot happening in Hopewell Creek."

"I'm sure it seems that way to a newcomer," Rosalind said with a delicate shrug. "When you've lived here all your life as I have, one church picnic or quilting circle blends into the next."

Beth couldn't help but detect a hint of condescension. "Each community has its own rhythm of life. I find Hopewell Creek quite appealing."

"How diplomatic," Rosalind observed. "I imagine it's quite different from St. Louis."

"Yes, though both have their merits."

Rosalind adjusted her gloves, studying Beth with undisguised curiosity. "It must have been difficult, arriving with certain expectations only to have them... dashed."

The reference to Beth's mail-order bride situation was thinly veiled. Beth felt her cheeks warm, but kept her composure. "Life rarely follows our anticipated path. The challenge is adapting gracefully to unexpected turns."

"Indeed," Rosalind murmured. "And how fortunate that Ezra offered you this position so quickly. He has such a compassionate nature."

Before Beth could respond, the office door opened, and Ezra entered, removing his hat as he stepped inside. He stopped short, clearly surprised to find the two women engaged in conversation.

"Rosalind," he said. "I wasn't expecting you."

"I wanted to ensure you remembered the Literary Society meeting this evening," Rosalind replied, rising gracefully. "And to verify you received the Emerson essay I sent over. It's central to our discussion."

"Yes to both," Ezra assured her, hanging his hat on the rack. "Though I may be somewhat late. Thursday is our busiest day for news gathering."

"We'll wait for you, of course," Rosalind said warmly. "Your insights are always valuable to our discussions." She turned to Beth with a practiced smile. "You're welcome to attend as well, Miss Beaumont. Do you enjoy Emerson's work?"

"I've read several of his essays," Beth answered truthfully. "His perspectives on self-reliance and nature are particularly thought-provoking."

Something flickered in Rosalind's eyes—perhaps surprise or reassessment. "Well, we meet at seven at my family's home. Nothing terribly formal." She turned back to Ezra. "Father mentioned you'll be stopping by the bank this afternoon?"

"Yes, after we sort through today's news items," Ezra confirmed.

"Excellent. I'll let him know to expect you." With a final smile at Ezra and a polite nod to Beth, Rosalind departed, leaving a lingering scent of expensive perfume in her wake.

Ezra watched the door close before turning to Beth with a rueful expression. "I should have warned you about potential visitors while I was gone."

"It was no trouble," Beth assured him, though she felt relieved by Rosalind's departure. "Miss Fairfield was perfectly civil."

Ezra gave her a knowing look. "Rosalind is always perfectly civil. It's one of her most effective weapons." He moved to his desk, removing his jacket. "How was your news gathering?"

Grateful for the change of subject, Beth presented her notes, detailing the various announcements and events she'd collected. Ezra listened attentively, occasionally nodding or asking clarifying questions.

"This is excellent work," he said when she finished. "You've gathered more in one morning than Marjorie typically managed in a full day."

The praise warmed Beth. "People were very forthcoming once I mentioned the Herald."

"The newspaper holds a special place in community life," Ezra agreed. "Now, let me share what I learned from the outlying areas."

Ezra's news from the farms included reports of promising crop conditions, a new irrigation method one farmer was implementing with success, and the birth of triplet calves at the Wilson ranch—a rare occurrence deemed almost miraculous by the rancher's wife.

"The Wilsons are inviting people to come see the calves on Sunday after church," Ezra explained. "Mrs. Wilson is convinced it's a divine sign of prosperity for Hopewell Creek."

"Is it?" Beth asked, curious about his perspective.

Ezra smiled. "I'm not qualified to interpret divine signs, but it certainly makes for an interesting local story. We'll give it prominent placement."

They spent the next hour organizing their collected news items, determining which deserved longer articles and which would be brief mentions. Beth marveled at Ezra's editorial instincts—his ability to discern what would interest readers most and how to present information effectively.

"The railroad piece will be our lead article," he decided, sketching a rough layout. "Then the farm report, school recitation program, and church announcements. Smaller items can fill the remaining spaces."

"What about advertisements?" Beth asked.

"Those are already set from last week, though we should leave space for the Singer sewing machines. Mr. O'Leary will want to promote those." He glanced up at Beth. "You have a good eye for organization. Would you like to try designing the layout for the community announcements section?"

The offer surprised and pleased her. "I'd be happy to try."

"Good. We'll work on that after lunch." He checked the wall clock. "Speaking of which, it's well past noon. Are you hungry?"

"Now that you mention it, yes," Beth admitted.

"Let me buy you lunch at the café as thanks for your excellent work this morning," Ezra suggested, rising from his desk.

Chapter 13

They walked to the O'Leary Café, where the midday rush had already subsided. Mrs. O'Leary greeted them warmly and seated them at the same window table they'd occupied yesterday.

"Special today is chicken and dumplings," she announced. "Made them extra fluffy, just how you like, Ezra."

"You know my weaknesses too well," Ezra said with a smile. "That sounds perfect. Beth?"

"The same for me, please," Beth agreed.

As Mrs. O'Leary bustled away, Ezra turned to Beth. "I wanted to ask—are you interested in attending the Literary Society meeting tonight? You certainly shouldn't feel obligated by Rosalind's invitation."

Beth considered this. "I do enjoy literary discussions, but..." she hesitated.

"But you're concerned about navigating an unfamiliar social situation?" Ezra suggested perceptively.

"Yes, partly that," Beth acknowledged. "And I'm not certain Miss Fairfield's invitation was entirely sincere."

Ezra's expression turned thoughtful. "Rosalind can be... territorial about the Literary Society. She founded it last year after returning from a year at a finishing school in Boston. It's primarily attended by the more... affluent townspeople."

"I see," Beth said, understanding the social dynamics at play.

"That said," Ezra continued, "the discussions are usually stimulating, and you clearly have an appreciation for literature. You'd contribute valuable perspectives."

"Perhaps another time," Beth decided. "It doesn't really sound like something I would enjoy. I much prefer to stay in this evening and sew. And truthfully, I'm still adjusting to all the changes of the past few days."

Ezra nodded. "A reasonable choice. The society meets monthly—there will be other opportunities."

Their food arrived, steaming and aromatic. The dumplings were indeed remarkably light, floating atop a rich chicken broth with tender morsels of meat and vegetables.

"This is wonderful," Beth said after her first bite.

"Mrs. O'Leary's chicken and dumplings are legendary," Ezra agreed. "People have been known to travel from neighboring towns just for a bowl."

As they ate, their conversation turned to the newspaper business. Beth found herself fascinated by Ezra's knowledge of journalism and printing.

"How did you learn all the technical aspects of running a newspaper?" she asked. "The typesetting, printing, layout—it seems incredibly complex."

"Trial and error, mostly," Ezra admitted. "When I purchased the Herald from Mr. Thatcher, he gave me a week's training on the press before heading east to live with his daughter. The first few editions under my management had some rather embarrassing errors."

"Such as?"

Ezra's eyes crinkled with amusement. "In my third week, I accidentally transposed two lines in a wedding announcement. Instead of stating that 'Miss Henson and Mr. Cooper were joined in holy matrimony,' it read that 'Miss Henson and Mr. Cooper were joined in holy macaroni.'"

Beth couldn't suppress her laughter. "Oh, no! How did they react?"

"Fortunately, they had a sense of humor about it. They even saved that copy of the paper to show their grandchildren someday." He took a sip of water. "But it taught me to proofread everything twice, especially important announcements."

"Have there been other memorable mistakes?" Beth asked, enjoying this glimpse of Ezra's early career struggles.

"More than I care to admit," he confessed. "Once, in an article about the town council meeting, I meant to write that 'the council debated the issue.' Somehow it came out as 'the council defeated the bishop.'"

Beth's shoulders shook with suppressed laughter. "What did the bishop think of that?"

"He suggested I might benefit from additional prayer," Ezra said with a straight face before breaking into a smile himself.

Their shared laughter felt comfortable and natural. There was something about Ezra's company that put her at ease, despite the professional nature of their relationship.

"The Herald seems like such an important part of the community's identity," Beth observed as they finished their meal. "You've created something truly meaningful here."

"I'm merely its current steward," Ezra said modestly. "Newspapers, like communities, outlast individuals. But I do hope I've contributed something worthwhile to Hopewell Creek."

As they walked back to the Herald office, Beth noticed how people greeted Ezra—with genuine respect and warmth. He knew everyone by name, asked after family members, remembered details from previous conversations. This wasn't merely professional courtesy, but authentic connection.

Later that afternoon, while Ezra visited the bank to meet with Mr. Fairfield, Beth was alone in the quiet office. Sunlight streamed through the windows, illuminating the orderly chaos of newsprint, ink, and the tools of their trade. She ran her fingers lightly over the typesetting tray, marveling at how quickly this place had begun to feel familiar.

Just three days ago, she'd arrived in Hopewell Creek, heartbroken and desperate. Now she sat at her own desk, with meaningful work and the beginnings of a place in this community. The thought filled her with a quiet gratitude that bordered on wonder.

But it wasn't just the work or the town that had begun to transform her outlook. It was Ezra himself—his quiet integrity, his kindness without condescension, his belief in her abilities. She found herself anticipating his return from the bank, missing his presence in the office.

Beth paused in her work, startled by the realization. This growing warmth she felt in his company, the way her spirits lifted when he entered a room—these feelings extended beyond professional admiration or even friendship.

"Oh," she whispered to the empty office, the truth dawning with gentle clarity. She was beginning to care for Ezra Simmons in a way she hadn't expected—a way that both frightened and exhilarated her.

Chapter 14

Beth smoothed her skirts and adjusted the basket on her arm as she approached the church. In the basket, she carried her sewing kit, a few spools of thread, a thimble, and needles.

Women's voices carried through the open windows, interspersed with laughter. Beth hesitated at the bottom of the steps, a familiar tightness constricting her chest. The last time she'd participated in a ladies' gathering had been nearly four years ago, before her parents' decline had accelerated and their family's standing in the community had withered. She'd forgotten the particular blend of anticipation and anxiety such social occasions could evoke.

"You're right on time," called a cheerful voice.

Beth looked up to see Maggie O'Leary descending the church steps, her freckled face alight with a welcoming smile.

"I was just stepping out to see if anyone else was coming up the road," Maggie explained. "Come on in—we're just getting set up."

Taking a fortifying breath, Beth climbed the steps alongside the vivacious young woman.

"I've hope my skills will be adequate today," Beth said.

Maggie linked her arm through Beth's. "Don't you worry about that. Some ladies come just for the conversation, and their stitches are so crooked, Pastor Paul jokes they're writing in tongues."

Beth couldn't help laughing at this irreverent description, and with that small release of tension, she allowed Maggie to guide her into the church.

The interior had been transformed. The pews had been pushed to the sides, and 1 large quilting frame dominated the center of the room. Chairs had been arranged around it. Women of varying ages busied themselves arranging fabric scraps, threading needles, and chatting animatedly.

"Look who I found," Maggie announced to the room at large.

Heads turned, and Beth felt a momentary self-consciousness as she became the center of attention.

Mrs. Jenkins bustled over immediately. "Beth, dear! I'm so glad you decided to join us." She turned to the room. "Ladies, this is Beth Beaumont, my newest boarder."

A chorus of greetings rose up, and Beth recognized several faces—Mrs. O'Leary from the café, Mary Hawthorne, the pastor's wife, and others she'd seen in passing during her brief time in Hopewell Creek.

"Come meet everyone properly," Mrs. Jenkins urged, guiding Beth around the circle.

There was elderly Mrs. Anders with arthritic hands that somehow still produced the finest stitch work in the county; plump and jovial Mrs. Bellwether, the blacksmith's wife; stern-faced but kind-hearted Mrs. Turner, the milliner and owner of the dressmaking shop; shy young Sarah Collins, who'd recently married the apothecary; and several others whose names Beth carefully committed to memory.

Noticeably absent was Rosalind Fairfield.

"We're working on Sadie Peterson's wedding quilt," explained Mrs. Hawthorne as she showed Beth to a seat around the quilting frame.

The quilt stretched before Beth was a gorgeous wedding ring pattern. The border featured intricate appliquéd vines and flowers.

"It's beautiful," Beth said with genuine admiration, running her fingertips lightly over the fabric.

"We've been working on it for months now. We just need to quilt it," Mrs. Hawthorne said proudly.

"Where would you like me to start?" Beth asked, opening her sewing basket and selecting a needle.

"Anywhere you'd like," Mrs. Turner said. "Have you quilted before?"

"I have, though it's been some time," Beth admitted.

She threaded her needle with ease and began to work. The rhythm of needle and thread was soothing. As she worked, the conversation flowed around her like a gentle stream.

"Sarah, how is that husband of yours adjusting to married life?" asked Mrs. O'Leary with good-natured nosiness.

Sarah Collins blushed. "Very well, ma'am. Though he still can't understand how I can drink a full pot of coffee before breakfast."

"Men never do understand a woman's need for fortification before facing the day," Mrs. Bellwether declared, prompting knowing laughter from around the circle.

Beth smiled as she worked, gradually joining the conversation when questions were directed her way, mostly about her journey to Hopewell Creek and her impressions of the town.

"And how are you finding your work at the Herald?" Mrs. Turner asked as she snipped a thread.

Beth felt all eyes turn toward her with interest.

"It's been a wonderful," she replied honestly. "Mr. Simmons has been very patient in teaching me the business."

"Ezra Simmons is a fine young man," pronounced Mrs. Anders, her needle flashing in the light streaming through the windows. "His father is just the same—backbone of integrity."

"Ezra is quite handsome, too," Maggie added with a mischievous grin. "Don't you think, Beth?"

Beth felt heat rising in her cheeks. "He's been a very kind employer," she said carefully.

"Just an employer, is he?" teased Mrs. Bellwether, exchanging knowing glances with Mrs. Jenkins.

"That's quite enough, ladies," Mrs. Hawthorne interjected, though her eyes twinkled. "Let's not embarrass our newcomer."

The conversation mercifully shifted to other topics—the unseasonably warm weather for April, predictions for the harvest, and plans for the upcoming summer festival in June.

Beth returned her attention to her stitching, grateful for the reprieve. As her needle dipped in and out of the fabric, creating tiny perfect stitches around the curve of a rose petal on the border of the quilt, she reflected on the unexpected direction her life had taken. Just over a week ago, she'd been trapped in misery, and now...

Now she sat among kind women, contributing to a beautiful work for a soon-to-be bride. She had meaningful employment and the beginnings of friendship. The stark contrast brought a lump to her throat, and she blinked rapidly to dispel sudden tears.

"That's lovely work, dear," said Mrs. Anders softly beside her, nodding at Beth's stitches. "You have a genuine gift."

"Thank you," Beth replied. "My grandmother taught me when I was young. She always said that every stitch should be made with love."

"A wise woman, your grandmother," Mrs. Turner said approvingly. "I can see her lessons took root."

After about an hour of work, Mrs. O'Leary and Maggie unveiled refreshments—fragrant cinnamon rolls and a large pot of coffee. The women happily abandoned their needles to gather around a table at the back of the church.

"Beth, tell us about St. Louis," Maggie urged, as they enjoyed their treats. "I've never been to a big city."

"It's quite different from Hopewell Creek," Beth said, considering how to describe her former home without revealing the painful aspects of her departure. "Much noisier, with streetcars and carriages at all hours. The buildings are taller, and there are gaslight lamps along the main streets."

"Did you attend many fancy parties?" Sarah asked wistfully. "I've read about city balls in novels."

Beth smiled gently. "Some, a few years ago. Though they're rarely as romantic as novels suggest. Mostly a great deal of uncomfortable shoes and conversations about the weather."

This prompted chuckles around the group.

"And what brought you to our little corner of Colorado?" Mrs. Turner asked, her sharp eyes studying Beth's face.

Beth hesitated, uncertain how much to reveal. "I was seeking a change," she said finally. "An opportunity for a fresh start."

Something in her tone must have conveyed that further probing would be unwelcome, for Mrs. Hawthorne smoothly intervened.

"And we're delighted you've found your way to us," she said warmly. "Especially Ezra, I imagine. That poor man had been running himself ragged trying to manage the Herald alone."

"He does seem very dedicated to his work," Beth said, grateful for the shift in focus.

"The Herald is more than just his livelihood," Mrs. Jenkins explained. "When Ezra took it over after Mr. Thatcher left, the paper was failing. Everyone said a young man with no experience couldn't possibly make it work."

"But he proved them wrong," Mrs. Bellwether continued. "Turned it into the voice of Hopewell Creek. During the drought two years ago, he used the paper to coordinate relief efforts, connect those in need with those who could help."

"He takes his responsibility to the community very seriously," Mrs. Hawthorne added. "Perhaps too seriously at times. He rarely takes a day for himself."

"My Tom says Ezra works harder than any three men," Mrs. Bellwether said proudly, as though Ezra's industriousness reflected well on the entire town.

Beth found herself absorbing these details eagerly, piecing together a fuller picture of the man who had offered her such timely salvation.

"Enough about Ezra Simmons," Mrs. Turner declared. "Beth, I'd be interested in seeing you at my shop sometime. I could use a skilled hand with fine stitch work, if you ever find yourself wanting additional employment."

"Thank you," Beth said, surprised and pleased by the offer. "That's very kind."

"Not kind at all," Mrs. Turner corrected briskly. "Purely practical. Good seamstresses are hard to find in these parts."

With refreshments finished, the women returned to their quilting. The conversation continued to flow, ranging from practical matters like preserving techniques and laundry methods to local gossip.

"Did you hear about the Wilcox family cow?" Mrs. O'Leary asked as she carefully stitched a blue square.

"The one that wandered into Mr. Harding's feed store?" Mrs. Jenkins replied. "Ate half a bag of oats before they could get her out!"

"Poor Harding was beside himself," Mrs. Bellwether added with a chuckle. "Said he'd never seen a cow with such expensive taste."

Beth laughed along, the simple joy of feminine camaraderie washing over her like a healing balm. Here, there were no judgments about her family's failures, no whispers about gambling debts or disgrace. She was simply Beth, a newcomer with a talent for fine stitchery and a willing pair of hands.

As the afternoon progressed, Beth's confidence grew. She volunteered suggestions for the border pattern, demonstrated a particular stitch technique her grandmother had taught her, and even shared an anecdote about a disastrous attempt at quilting when she was twelve. This had resulted in her accidentally sewing her project to her skirt.

By the time they began packing up their supplies around five o'clock, Beth felt a genuine connection with these women. It wasn't yet friendship—that would take time and trust—but it was acceptance, a tentative welcome into their circle.

"You'll come next Saturday, won't you?" Maggie asked as they folded the completed sections of the quilt.

"I'd like that very much," Beth replied sincerely.

"And we expect to see you at service tomorrow," Mrs. Hawthorne added. "Pastor Paul has been preparing a wonderful sermon on new beginnings."

"I wouldn't miss it," Beth assured her. The prospect of attending church—something she'd been unable to do regularly during her parents' decline—filled her with anticipation.

Mrs. Jenkins approached as the other women began departing. "Will you walk back with me, dear? Or did you have other plans for the afternoon?"

"I thought I might explore the town a bit more before returning," Beth said. "While the weather is so pleasant."

"A fine idea," Mrs. Jenkins approved. "Hopewell Creek shines its brightest on Saturday afternoons. Everyone's finished their week's work and is in good spirits. Do join us for supper, though—I'm making chicken pot pie."

"That sounds wonderful," Beth said gratefully.

With final goodbyes exchanged and promises to meet again tomorrow at church, Beth stepped out into the late afternoon sunshine. The quilting circle had lasted longer than she'd expected, but the hours had passed in pleasant industry and conversation.

She decided to walk down Main Street, enjoying the bustle of weekend activity. Farmers and ranchers from outlying homesteads had come to town for supplies, families strolled along the boardwalks, and the general atmosphere was one of relaxed sociability.

Beth observed everything with new eyes. These weren't just buildings and strangers anymore—they were becoming familiar, part of a community she might someday claim as her own. Mrs. Turner's dressmaking shop with its display of fashionable bonnets; the general store where Maggie's father greeted customers with a booming laugh; Jonas Miller's law office with its polished brass nameplate.

And there, in the heart of town, the Hopewell Creek Herald. Beth paused outside, studying the building where she'd found an unexpected purpose. The office was closed for the weekend, but she could picture Ezra inside. The thought brought an unbidden smile to her lips.

"Planning to break in and steal all the news secrets?" came an amused voice behind her.

Beth turned to find Ezra himself approaching, a parcel under his arm. He wore casual attire today—a simple shirt without a tie, sleeves rolled up against the afternoon warmth, and a less formal vest. The effect was oddly disarming.

"Mr. Simmons," she said, flustered at being caught daydreaming outside their workplace. "I was just passing by after the quilting circle."

"Ah, yes, the famous Saturday quilting circle," he said, stopping beside her. "Did you enjoy yourself?"

"Very much," Beth replied. "Everyone was welcoming, and the quilt so far is impressive."

"They're a remarkable group of women," Ezra agreed.

"You're not working today?" Beth asked, noting the parcel under his arm that appeared to contain books.

"Not at the moment," he admitted. "Though I did spend the morning finalizing the layout for Monday. I've just come from Prescott's Bookshop—my one indulgence each month is a new volume or two."

"What did you select?" Beth asked, genuinely curious.

Ezra shifted the parcel to reveal the titles: a collection of Mark Twain's writings and a newer novel Beth wasn't familiar with.

"Do you enjoy reading fiction?" she asked, somewhat surprised. He struck her as a man more likely to read histories or political treatises.

"I do," he said, a hint of defensiveness in his tone. "A good story can reveal truths about humanity that facts alone cannot convey."

"I couldn't agree more," Beth said warmly. "My father used to say—" She stopped abruptly, the memory catching her unawares.

Ezra waited, his expression encouraging.

"My father used to say that fiction was truth wearing a mask," she continued after a moment. "Before... well, before things changed."

Something in Ezra's eyes suggested he understood there was more to that statement, but he didn't press.

"A wise observation," he said instead. "Are you heading back to Mrs. Jenkins? I could walk with you part of the way."

Beth nodded, grateful for his tact. "That would be nice, though I'm in no hurry. It's such a beautiful afternoon."

They fell into step together, walking at a leisurely pace. Beth was acutely aware of Ezra beside her, his tall frame keeping a respectful distance but close enough that occasionally their shoulders nearly brushed. Several townspeople greeted them as they passed, and Beth noticed curious glances directed their way.

"I should warn you," Ezra said, apparently noticing the same thing, "walking with me may subject you to town gossip. Small communities can be rather...enthusiastic about interpreting social interactions."

"I survived the quilting circle interrogation," Beth replied with a small smile. "I believe I can weather a few curious glances."

Ezra chuckled. "Ah, so they've already begun their questioning."

Beth felt her cheeks warm. "Something along those lines," she admitted.

"My apologies," he said, looking genuinely contrite. "They mean well, but subtlety isn't a community strength."

"There's no need to apologize," Beth assured him. "They were all very kind, and I enjoyed their company immensely."

They continued walking, their conversation turning to the upcoming edition of the Herald. Ezra described several stories he was developing, and Beth offered suggestions about the layout. It was easy, comfortable—the boundary between employer and employee softening into something more like partnership.

As they neared the intersection where their paths would diverge—Ezra toward his home on Oak Street, Beth toward Mrs. Jenkins' boarding house—neither seemed eager to end the encounter.

"Will you be attending service tomorrow?" Ezra asked, pausing at the corner.

"Yes," Beth nodded. "I'm looking forward to it."

"Would you care to walk with me?" he offered, then quickly added, "That is, if Mrs. Jenkins hasn't already claimed your company."

Beth felt a flutter of pleasure at the invitation. "That would be lovely."

"Excellent," Ezra said, looking pleased. "Shall I call for you at half-past nine?"

"I'll be ready," Beth promised.

They parted ways with polite goodbyes. Beth glanced back over her shoulder as Ezra continued down Oak Street. He must have felt her gaze, for he turned and raised his hand in a final farewell before disappearing around a corner.

Chapter 15

Beth stood before the small mirror in her room, pinning the last strands of her honey-blonde hair into place. She stepped back to examine her appearance, smoothing down the front of her Sunday dress—one of the donated garments, but the finest among everything she owned. The deep blue calico complemented her eyes, and though it wasn't fashionable by St. Louis standards, it was clean, pressed, and respectable.

A knock at the front door downstairs sent a flutter through her stomach. Ezra had arrived precisely when promised. Beth reached for her small Bible, took a steadying breath, and headed downstairs.

Mrs. Jenkins had beaten her to the door and was already engaged in animated conversation with Ezra when Beth descended the staircase.

"There she is," Mrs. Jenkins announced, turning with a knowing smile. "Doesn't she look lovely this morning?"

Ezra, dressed in a crisp dark suit with a neatly pressed white shirt and blue tie, turned toward Beth. His eyes widened slightly, and he removed his hat.

"Good morning, Miss Beaumont," he said, his voice warm. "You look... very nice."

The hesitation in his compliment suggested he'd initially thought of a more effusive word, but had chosen a safer alternative. Beth felt her cheeks warm under his appreciative gaze.

"Thank you, Mr. Simmons. You're right on time."

"Always, when something matters," he replied, then cleared his throat. "Shall we? It's a fine morning for a walk."

Mrs. Jenkins handed Beth a shawl. "The air still has a nip this early," she said. "I'll see you both at service."

Beth wrapped the light shawl around her shoulders and stepped outside into the clear morning light. The sky stretched in an endless azure expanse above them, unmarred by clouds.

"Did you sleep well?" Ezra asked as they set off down the path.

"Very well, thank you," Beth replied. "And you?"

"Well enough, though I stayed up rather later than intended with my new books."

Beth smiled. "Was Mr. Twain that compelling?"

"He was," Ezra admitted with a chuckle. "I confess, the novel that kept me awake. I kept telling myself 'just one more chapter' until I realized the hour was quite indecent."

"I understand completely. Books have a way of making time disappear."

They walked toward the church, the sounds of other churchgoers ahead and behind them on the road. Families with children in their Sunday best, elderly couples walking arm-in-arm, young men with freshly slicked hair and nervous expressions.

"May I ask you something, Miss Beaumont?" Ezra said suddenly.

"Of course."

"What was your favorite book as a child?"

The question surprised Beth, both in its unexpectedness and its innocence. She thought for a moment before answering.

"'Little Women,'" she said finally. "My mother read it to my brother and me when I was eight. I so wanted to be Jo—brave and literary and unafraid to speak her mind."

Ezra nodded appreciatively. "A fine choice. I imagine you have quite a bit of Jo March in you, coming all this way on your own."

Beth hadn't considered that comparison. "Perhaps, though with considerably less success at writing stories. And yours? What book captured young Ezra Simmons' imagination?"

"'Robinson Crusoe,'" he answered without hesitation. "I was fascinated by the idea of building a life from nothing, creating order from chaos. I constructed quite an elaborate fort in our barn that summer, much to my father's dismay when he discovered I'd repurposed several essential tools."

Beth laughed, picturing a young, serious-faced Ezra industriously building his refuge.

"My father wasn't nearly as understanding as Crusoe's author," Ezra continued, smiling at the memory. "I spent the next week mucking out stalls as penance."

"A harsh but effective lesson in respecting other people's property, I imagine."

"Indeed. Though it didn't cure my love of building things. Just redirected it toward more... approved materials."

The church came into view ahead of them, its white steeple rising against the blue sky. People streamed toward it from all directions, converging like tributaries feeding a river.

"I should warn you," Ezra said, his voice dropping slightly, "my mother will almost certainly be here today. She makes the effort for Sunday services whenever her health permits."

"I look forward to meeting her," Beth said honestly.

"She'll have a thousand questions," he warned. "She worries I spend too much time alone with my newspapers and books."

"A mother's prerogative, I believe."

As they approached the church steps, several people called greetings to Ezra, who returned them with friendly nods and responses. Beth noticed the subtle shift in his demeanor—slightly more formal, consciously fitting the role of newspaper editor and respected community member.

"Ezra! Good morning!"

An older man with silver-streaked dark hair and Ezra's distinctive jawline approached them. Jacob Simmons moved with the easy confidence of a man comfortable in his own skin, dressed in a well-worn but immaculately clean suit.

"Morning, Pa," Ezra replied warmly. "You remember Miss Beaumont?"

"Indeed, I do," Jacob said, tipping his hat to Beth. "A pleasure to see you again, young lady. I trust my son is treating you fairly at that newspaper of his?"

"More than fairly, sir," Beth assured him. "I'm fortunate to have found such agreeable employment."

"She's being modest," Ezra interjected. "She's already proving invaluable. Her eye for detail has saved us from at least three embarrassing typographical errors."

"Then we're all in your debt, Miss Beaumont," Jacob said with a wink. "Nothing worse than opening the Herald to find the church social announced as a 'scared supper' instead of a 'sacred supper,' as happened once before my son became more vigilant."

"That was not my error," Ezra protested. "That was Mr. Thatcher's doing, when he was training me."

"Of course, son," Jacob said with exaggerated agreement. "Come along. Your mother's already inside, saving our usual pew."

They followed Jacob into the church, the cool interior a marked contrast to the warming day outside. Sunlight filtered through the simple stained-glass windows, casting colored patterns across the wooden pews and floor. The church was nearly full, the congregation a sea of Sunday best attire, voices humming in pre-service conversation.

Jacob led them to a pew about halfway down the center aisle, where a slender woman with silver-streaked dark hair sat waiting. When she saw their approach, her face brightened with a smile that transformed her somewhat pale features into striking beauty.

"There you are," she said as Jacob slid in beside her. Her voice was soft but clear. "I was beginning to wonder about you." Her observant gaze moved past her husband to Ezra, then settled with undisguised interest on Beth.

"Mother, may I present Miss Beth Beaumont," Ezra said formally. "Miss Beaumont, my mother, Mrs. Evelyn Simmons."

"How do you do, Mrs. Simmons," Beth said, offering a polite nod.

Evelyn studied Beth's face with keen interest. "So you're the young lady who's been saving my son from drowning in printer's ink. It's a pleasure to finally meet you."

"The pleasure is mine," Beth replied.

"Do join us," Evelyn said, moving slightly to create space on the pew. "There's plenty of room."

Beth hesitated, not wanting to intrude on their family tradition.

"Please," Ezra added quietly. "Unless you'd prefer to sit elsewhere?"

"Not at all," Beth said, feeling strangely moved by the simple invitation. "Thank you."

They settled into the pew, Beth acutely aware of Ezra beside her, his arm occasionally brushing against hers as he adjusted his position. The proximity stirred a warmth within her.

Evelyn leaned forward to speak across Ezra. "You must join us for dinner after service, Miss Beaumont. Nothing elaborate, but I would love to become better acquainted."

"That's very kind, but I wouldn't want to impose—"

"Nonsense," Evelyn interrupted gently. "Jacob has told me what a godsend you've been at the Herald. The least we can do is feed you a proper Sunday meal."

Ezra turned to Beth. "You'd be most welcome," he said. "Mother makes a roast beef that would make even the most hardened cattle rustler repent his ways."

Beth laughed softly. "Well, in that case, how could I refuse?"

"Excellent," Evelyn said with satisfaction. "You can ride out with Ezra in his buggy. It's not far—just a few miles east of town."

Pastor Paul stepped to the pulpit, and a reverent hush fell over the congregation. The service began with a familiar hymn; the congregation rising to their feet as Mrs. Hawthorne played the opening notes on the small organ.

Beth sang with genuine fervor. Being in church again, surrounded by people united in worship, awakened something long dormant within her. She felt Ezra's voice beside her, a rich baritone that blended harmoniously with her own lighter tones.

As the congregation sat for the scripture reading, Beth couldn't help but notice several curious glances directed their way. She recognized Mrs. Turner's assessing gaze from across the aisle, and Rosalind Fairfield's barely concealed frown from three rows ahead.

The realization that she was being observed as Ezra Simmons' companion brought a strange mixture of discomfort and pride. She focused her attention firmly on Pastor Paul as he began to read from Isaiah.

"For I am about to do something new. See, I have already begun! Do you not see it? I will make a pathway through the wilderness. I will create rivers in the dry wasteland."

The words resonated deeply with Beth. A pathway through the wilderness. Wasn't that precisely what had been provided for her? When she had been most lost, most desperate, a way forward had appeared. First through the advertisement that brought her to Hopewell Creek, then through Ezra's timely offer of employment and support.

Pastor Paul's sermon explored the theme of new beginnings, of God's provision in unexpected places and forms. He spoke of wilderness periods in life—times of testing, of wandering, of uncertainty—and how these often preceded seasons of greatest growth and blessing.

"The Israelites wandered for forty years," he said, his voice rising and falling with the cadence of a practiced orator. "Forty years of hardship, of manna and quail, of water from rocks. But those wilderness years weren't wasted. They were preparation for the Promised Land. God was building a people who could properly steward the blessing He intended for them."

Beth felt the words sink deep into her soul. Perhaps her own wilderness years—watching her family disintegrate, struggling to maintain her faith amid disappointment and hardship—perhaps they too served a purpose. Perhaps they were preparing her for something yet to come.

She was so absorbed in these thoughts that she nearly missed the gentle touch on her arm. Ezra was offering her his hymnal, open to the page for the closing song. Their fingers brushed as she accepted it, and Beth felt that same surprising jolt of awareness she'd experienced in the newspaper office.

Their eyes met briefly, and something in Ezra's gaze suggested he might have felt it too.

The service concluded with a benediction, and the congregation began to disperse, the formal quiet giving way to the cheerful buzz of community fellowship. Beth followed the Simmons family into the churchyard, where clusters of people stood chatting in the mid-morning sunshine.

"Beth!"

Beth turned to see Maggie O'Leary approaching, her Sunday dress a cheerful yellow that matched her personality.

"Good morning, Maggie," Beth greeted her.

"Wasn't the sermon wonderful?" Maggie said, her eyes bright. "It felt as though Pastor Paul was speaking directly to me." She nodded politely to Ezra and his parents before continuing in a lower voice to Beth, "Will you be joining us for lunch at the café? Several of us gather there after service."

"Thank you, but I've been invited to dine with the Simmons family today," Beth explained.

Maggie's eyebrows rose in interest, but before she could comment, her mother called her away to help welcome a visiting family.

"Miss Beaumont."

The cool, precise voice cut through the general chatter. Beth turned to find Rosalind Fairfield standing before her, impeccably dressed in a fashionable dress of lavender silk that must have come from Denver or even further east. Beside her stood her father, Walt Fairfield, his prosperity evident in his expensive suit and gold watch chain.

"Good morning, Miss Fairfield," Beth replied evenly.

"I trust you're adapting well to our little community," Rosalind said, her smile not quite reaching her eyes. "It must be quite different from your previous... circumstances."

The slight emphasis conveyed volumes, and Beth realized that Rosalind was deliberately referencing her mail-order bride situation.

"Everyone has been most welcoming," Beth responded, refusing to be baited. "Hopewell Creek is fortunate to have such kind residents."

"Indeed," Walt Fairfield interjected, his gaze moving past Beth to where Ezra stood conversing with his father and another man. "Some more than others." He nodded toward Beth. "Miss Beaumont, I assume your position at the Herald is going well."

"Yes, it is."

"A fortuitous arrangement for both of you, I'm sure," he said, his tone inscrutable. "One hopes you'll remember that a newspaper carries significant responsibility in a community like ours. The power to shape opinion is not to be taken lightly."

Beth wondered at the veiled warning beneath his words. "Mr. Simmons has made that very clear, sir. He takes the Herald's integrity quite seriously."

"As well he should," Fairfield replied. "Well, good day to you, Miss Beaumont. Rosalind, shall we?"

With a final assessing look, Rosalind followed her father toward their waiting carriage, her back straight as a ruler.

Beth had little time to ponder this strange interaction as Ezra approached, having concluded his conversation.

"Ready to go?" he asked.

"Yes, whenever you are," Beth replied.

They bid farewell to Jacob and Evelyn.

"We'll see you there shortly," Ezra promised as he and Beth started toward town.

"Your mother is lovely," Beth said once they were out of earshot. "I can see where you get your thoughtfulness."

Ezra smiled. "And my stubbornness, though she'd never admit it. She taught school before her health declined. She has a mind like a steel trap and a heart to match."

"Her illness—is it serious?" Beth asked carefully.

"It comes and goes," Ezra explained, his expression sobering. "The fever that took my sister damaged Mother's lungs. Some days are better than others. Today seems to be one of the good ones, thankfully."

They walked in silence for a moment, Beth sensing Ezra's reluctance to dwell on painful memories.

"I noticed you were deep in thought during Pastor Paul's sermon," he said after a while.

Beth nodded. "It resonated with me. The idea that difficult seasons serve a purpose... it's comforting."

"It is," Ezra agreed. "Though I confess I've sometimes questioned the length of certain wilderness periods." His wry smile suggested personal experience with such questioning.

"I suppose we rarely recognize the boundaries of the wilderness while we're in it," Beth mused. "It's only in hindsight that we can see where the desert ended, and the promised land began."

Ezra looked at her with new appreciation. "That's remarkably insightful, Miss Beaumont. You might have a future writing editorials."

Beth laughed. "I think I'll master typesetting before aspiring to editorial wisdom."

They continued through town, which had a different character on Sunday mornings. Businesses were closed, the streets quieter than usual. Families walked together, some returning from church, others enjoying the fine weather.

Ezra led her down Oak Street, eventually stopping before a handsome two-story house setback from the road. A neat front yard with a few young trees and a welcoming porch created an immediate sense of home.

"This is yours?" Beth asked, admiring the well-maintained property.

"It is," Ezra replied, a note of pride in his voice. "I purchased it three years ago from the Widow Henderson when she moved to Denver to live with her daughter."

He led Beth up the short path to the porch, pausing to unlock the front door. "I apologize for not having time to tidy up. I rarely entertain visitors."

"Please, don't worry on my account," Beth assured him.

She followed him inside, immediately struck by the comfortable atmosphere. The front parlor was modestly but tastefully furnished, dominated by a large bookcase overflowing with volumes of all sizes. A writing desk sat near the window, papers neatly stacked upon it. The room had a distinctly masculine feel, yet wasn't sparse or unwelcoming.

"It's lovely," Beth said honestly. "Very... you."

Ezra's expression registered surprise, then pleasure. "Thank you. I'll just gather what we need for dinner and prepare the buggy. Feel free to look around while you wait."

As he disappeared through a doorway toward what Beth presumed was the kitchen, she wandered the parlor, drawn inevitably to the bookcase. The collection was impressive and eclectic—history volumes alongside poetry, scientific texts, well-worn classics and newer publications.

She ran her fingers lightly over the spines, reading titles and authors, forming a clearer picture of the man through his reading choices. One shelf held copies of newspapers from across the country—Denver, Chicago, even New York—suggesting Ezra's commitment to staying informed about journalism beyond Hopewell Creek.

On the mantel stood a few framed photographs. Beth recognized a younger Ezra in a family portrait, standing beside Jacob and Evelyn. Between them stood a young girl with a serious expression—Ellen, Beth guessed, the sister lost to fever.

"That was taken about a year before Ellen died," Ezra said quietly from the doorway. "She was eleven in the photo."

Beth turned, feeling as though she'd intruded on something private. "I'm sorry. I didn't mean to pry."

"Not at all," Ezra said, stepping into the room. "I put it there to be seen. To remember." He moved to stand beside her, looking at the photograph. "She was remarkably bright. Mother was certain she'd go to college, perhaps become a teacher like herself."

The sadness in his voice touched Beth deeply. She had experienced a similar loss with William's death. "It's important to remember," she said softly. "Even when it hurts."

Ezra nodded, then seemed to collect himself. "The buggy is ready whenever you are."

Beth followed him outside to where a neat one-horse buggy waited in the driveway beside the house. A sturdy bay horse stood patiently in the traces.

"This is Chester," Ezra said, patting the horse's neck. "The most reliable fellow in Hopewell Creek."

He helped Beth up into the buggy, his hand steady and warm on hers as she climbed in. The simple courtesy stirred something within her—how long had it been since anyone had treated her with such respectful consideration?

Ezra settled beside her, taking up the reins with practiced ease. "It's about two miles to the ranch," he explained as they set off. "The ride shouldn't take more than twenty minutes or so."

Chapter 16

Ezra and Beth left the neatly arranged streets of Hopewell Creek behind, following a well-maintained road that wound gently eastward. The landscape opened up around them—rolling grasslands dotted with wildflowers, stands of cottonwood trees marking the course of distant streams.

"It's beautiful," Beth said, taking in the vast openness. "So different from Missouri."

"Different beautiful, or just different?" Ezra asked, glancing at her.

"Beautiful," Beth confirmed. "There's something about this landscape that speaks of... possibility. As though you could become anyone out here, start fresh without the weight of the past."

"An apt description," Ezra agreed. "Though the past has a way of traveling with us, doesn't it? Even to the frontier."

The insight surprised Beth. "Yes," she admitted. "I'm finding that to be true."

"Not always a bad thing," Ezra added. "Some parts of our past are worth carrying forward."

Beth thought of her grandmother's lessons in sewing, her early love of reading fostered by her mother in better days, her brother's protective kindness. "Yes," she said. "Some parts definitely are."

The conversation flowed easily as they traveled, touching on topics from recent news to childhood memories. Beth found herself laughing more than she had in years at Ezra's dry observations and occasional self-deprecating stories about his early days running the newspaper.

"I once printed an entire edition with the date wrong," he admitted. "March 15 instead of May 15. Half the town showed up two months early for the festival."

Beth laughed. "What did you do?"

"Published a correction the next day and endured weeks of teasing about being 'the man who can't tell March from May,'" Ezra said ruefully. "Humility comes swiftly in small-town journalism."

As they crested a gentle rise, a sprawling property came into view. Fenced pastures stretched in all directions, dotted with grazing cattle. A large white farmhouse stood proudly at the center, surrounded by a cluster of outbuildings—barn, stables, bunkhouse, and what appeared to be a smokehouse.

"Welcome to Simmons Ranch," Ezra said as Beth took in the impressive operation.

"It's enormous," Beth said, unable to hide her awe. "I had no idea..."

"Pa started with just eighty acres and a dozen head of cattle," Ezra explained with evident pride. "Built it up year by year. Now we run over three hundred head on nearly a thousand acres."

"We?" Beth questioned, noting his use of the collective.

Ezra smiled sheepishly. "Old habit. I still think of it as 'ours,' though I haven't actively worked on the ranch since owning the Herald. I help during calving season and when they need an extra hand, but Pa has good men working for him now."

They approached the house along a tree-lined drive, and Beth saw Jacob Simmons emerge onto the broad front porch to greet them.

"Right on time," he called, as Ezra guided the buggy to a halt. "Your mother's been watching the road for the last fifteen minutes."

Ezra jumped down and came around to help Beth descend. As her feet touched the ground, Beth took in the house up close—two stories of solid construction, with a wide, welcoming porch that wrapped around one side. Flower boxes beneath the windows added a homey touch to the otherwise practical structure.

Jacob led them inside, where delicious aromas of roasting meat and baking bread filled the air. The interior was spacious and comfortable, with solid furniture that spoke of quality rather than ostentation. Family photographs and handmade quilts adorned the walls, creating a sense of history and belonging.

Evelyn emerged from the kitchen, wiping her hands on an apron. "Perfect timing," she said warmly. "Beth, would you like to freshen up before dinner? There's a washroom just down that hall."

"Thank you," Beth said gratefully, following Evelyn's directions.

When she returned, she found Ezra and his father deep in conversation about cattle prices, while Evelyn made final preparations in the kitchen. Without hesitation, Beth joined her.

"May I help with anything, Mrs. Simmons?"

Evelyn looked up in surprise, then smiled. "Most certainly. Would you mind setting the table? The dishes are in that cabinet there, and the silverware is in the drawer beneath it."

Beth set to work, arranging the plates and utensils on the large oak dining table, while Evelyn transferred vegetables from the stove to serving dishes.

"Ezra tells me you're quite skilled with the typesetting," Evelyn remarked, her tone conversational.

"I'm still learning, but I enjoy the precision it requires," Beth replied.

"That doesn't surprise me," Evelyn said, glancing approvingly at Beth's careful arrangement of the place settings. "You strike me as someone who appreciates order and attention to detail."

"I suppose I do," Beth acknowledged, somewhat surprised by the astute observation.

"Those are valuable traits, especially in a newspaper," Evelyn continued. "And in a home." There was a subtle emphasis on the last word that Beth didn't miss.

"Dinner's ready," Evelyn called to the men, smoothly changing the subject. "Jacob, would you carve the roast, please?"

The four of them gathered around the table, Jacob at one end, Evelyn at the other, with Beth and Ezra facing each other across the middle. Jacob offered a simple but heartfelt grace, and then the meal began in earnest.

The food was exceptional—tender roast beef, fluffy mashed potatoes, glazed carrots, and fresh-baked rolls that melted in Beth's mouth.

"So, Beth," Jacob said as he passed the potatoes, "tell us a bit about your family in St. Louis. Do you have brothers and sisters?"

"I had one brother, William. He passed away four years ago."

"I'm so sorry," Evelyn said softly, her expression genuinely sympathetic. "Was it sudden?"

"He was a soldier," Beth explained simply. "He died of wounds received at Fort—" She paused, her voice catching unexpectedly.

"You don't need to speak of it if it's painful," Jacob said kindly.

Beth shook her head. "It's all right. William was brave and honorable. He deserves to be remembered." She took a steadying breath.

"He's buried in a soldier's cemetery near the Mississippi. He was only twenty when he died."

"And your parents?" Evelyn asked.

"They… remain in St. Louis," she said.

Beth was grateful when Jacob steered the conversation to less personal topics, asking about her impressions of Colorado and her adjustment to life in Hopewell Creek.

"The landscape here is magnificent," Beth said with genuine enthusiasm. "So vast and open. And the people have been remarkably welcoming."

"Most of them, anyway," Ezra muttered, earning a sharp look from his mother.

"Hopewell Creek has its share of characters, like any town," Jacob acknowledged, "but at its heart, it's a community that looks after its own."

"And you're becoming one of our own, Beth," Evelyn added warmly. "Anyone who can save my son from working himself to exhaustion is welcome indeed."

"Mother," Ezra protested, though without real annoyance.

"Well, it's true," Evelyn insisted. "Jacob and I worry about you in that office day and night. Beth's arrival seems providential."

Beth felt a flush of pleasure at the implication that her presence mattered not just to Ezra, but to his family.

"I will say that having Miss Beaumont's assistance has made a significant difference for me." He glanced at Beth with approval that warmed her more.

After dinner, Jacob suggested they all move to the porch for coffee. The afternoon had grown pleasantly warm, with a gentle breeze stirring the leaves of the trees surrounding the house.

Settled in comfortable rocking chairs, they continued their conversation while watching the distant activities of the ranch—ranch hands moving between outbuildings, cattle grazing in the nearer pastures.

"Did Ezra mention that I used to teach?" Evelyn asked Beth, passing her a cup of coffee.

"He did," Beth replied. "He speaks very highly of your intellect."

Evelyn smiled fondly at her son. "Ezra was always my most eager student, even before formal schooling. He was reading by the age of three and writing his own little stories by the age of five."

"Stories that thankfully have been lost to history," Ezra interjected with a good-natured grimace.

"Not all of them," Jacob said with a wink. "Your mother has a box of them somewhere."

"Mother, you promised those would never see the light of day," Ezra said, looking genuinely alarmed.

Evelyn laughed, the sound girlish despite her years. "And they won't—unless absolutely necessary."

Beth watched this family teasing with a blend of enjoyment and wistfulness. It had been so long since her own family had engaged in such lighthearted banter.

"And what about you, Beth?" Evelyn asked. "Did you enjoy school?"

"Very much," Beth replied. "I had hoped to become a teacher myself, actually. I was fortunate to complete high school before—" She stopped, not wanting to mention the financial hardships that had prevented her from pursuing further education.

"Before circumstances intervened," Ezra finished for her diplomatically.

"Well, it's never too late," Evelyn said encouragingly. "Hopewell Creek's school is growing. They may need an assistant for Miss Preston before long."

"Mother, don't go arranging Beth's future just yet," Ezra said, though his tone was gentle. "She's only just settled into the Herald, and I wish to keep her employed with me."

"Of course, dear," Evelyn agreed, though she gave Beth a knowing look that suggested the subject might arise again.

The conversation turned to community matters—the upcoming summer festival, improvements needed at the church, and local families' news. Beth was struck by how thoroughly the Simmons were woven into the fabric of Hopewell Creek society, despite living outside town. They seemed to know everyone and take a genuine interest in the community's welfare.

As the afternoon progressed, Beth found herself increasingly comfortable in their company. Jacob shared stories of the ranch's early days, including misadventures with stubborn cattle and unpredictable weather. Evelyn spoke of her teaching years with evident passion, describing students who had gone on to college or established businesses in the region.

Throughout it all, Beth was aware of Ezra watching her when he thought she wouldn't notice, his expression thoughtful and, dare she think it, admiring?

Eventually, Ezra glanced at the sky and reluctantly announced, "We should probably start back soon. The light won't hold forever."

Beth hadn't realized how swiftly the time had passed. "Of course," she said, rising from her chair. "Mrs. Simmons, thank you for such a wonderful meal and delightful company."

"The pleasure was ours, dear," Evelyn said, taking Beth's hands in her own. "You must come again soon. Perhaps next Sunday?"

"I'd like that very much," Beth replied, touched by the invitation.

Jacob walked them to the buggy, helping Beth up while giving Ezra a few last-minute updates about ranch matters.

As they pulled away, Beth turned to wave to the couple standing arm-in-arm on the porch. They made a striking picture—strong, weathered Jacob and his slender, silver-haired wife, framed by the sturdy home they'd built together.

"Your parents are wonderful," Beth said once they were on the road. "Thank you for including me today."

"They're rather fond of you already," Ezra replied, a smile in his voice. "Particularly Mother. She's been trying to find me an intellectual equal for conversation for years."

Beth laughed. "Hardly equal. Your mother's knowledge puts me to shame. She's remarkably well read for—" She stopped, concerned she might sound disrespectful.

"For a frontier rancher's wife?" Ezra finished, glancing at her with amusement. "Mother would agree with you. She's maintained her subscription to three different literary journals and insists on having books ordered from as far as Boston. She believes education shouldn't end with marriage or motherhood."

"She's right," Beth said with conviction. "The mind needs nourishment, just as the body does."

Ezra studied her for a moment before returning his attention to the road. "You continue to surprise me, Miss Beaumont."

"How so?"

"Your resilience, for one thing. Your adaptability. Most women in your position might have been crushed by what happened with Dobbins. Yet here you are, building a new life with remarkable grace."

Beth considered this. "I'm not sure if it's grace so much as necessity," she said honestly. "Sometimes moving forward is the only choice."

"Perhaps," Ezra conceded. "But the manner of moving forward reveals character. You could have been bitter, resentful. Instead, you've embraced Hopewell Creek with an open heart."

The compliment warmed Beth, but she felt obliged to counter it with honesty. "I have my moments of doubt and fear," she admitted. "They just don't serve any useful purpose, so I try not to indulge them."

"A practical philosophy," Ezra said approvingly.

The buggy rolled along the road, the afternoon sunlight casting long shadows across the grassland. In the distance, the outline of Hopewell Creek took shape against the horizon.

Beth wished the journey could last longer. There was something intimate about sitting side by side in the buggy, the rhythmic clop of Chester's hooves and the creak of leather creating a peaceful backdrop to their conversation.

"Ezra," she began, then paused, realizing she'd used his given name for the first time.

He turned to her, eyebrows raised in question.

"I just wanted to say... thank you. Not just for today, but for everything since I arrived in Hopewell Creek. Your kindness has made all the difference."

Something shifted in his expression—a softening, a vulnerability she hadn't seen before.

"It's been my privilege," he said quietly. "Truly."

Their eyes held for a moment longer than strictly proper, and Beth felt that now-familiar flutter in her chest. Then Ezra turned his attention back to the road, but not before Beth caught the slight upward curve of his lips.

Chapter 17

Beth awoke the following Saturday to the persistent tapping of raindrops against her window. She pushed herself up on her elbows and watched rivulets of water streak down the glass. The sky beyond was a canvas of pewter and charcoal, promising a day of steady spring rain. She sighed and sank back against her pillow, recalling Mrs. Jenkins' announcement the previous evening that the church picnic would relocate to the community hall if rain persisted.

A sharp knock at her door jolted her from her reverie.

"Miss Beaumont? Are you awake?" Mrs. Jenkins called through the door.

"Yes, coming," Beth replied, swinging her legs over the side of the bed and hastily pulling on her wrapper.

She opened the door to find Mrs. Jenkins balancing a small tray with a steaming cup of coffee.

"Thought you might appreciate this on such a dreary morning," the older woman said, passing the cup to Beth. "I've got breakfast nearly ready downstairs when you're dressed."

"Thank you," Beth said, breathing in the rich aroma. "Has the rain been falling long?"

"Since before dawn, but it's lightening up. Pastor Paul sent word the social's still on—they've moved everything to the church hall."

"I wasn't sure if I should attend..." Beth began, uncertainty creeping into her voice.

Mrs. Jenkins placed her hands on her hips. "And why wouldn't you? You're as much a part of this community as anyone. Besides, your potato salad's chilling in my icebox. Can't let good food go to waste."

Beth smiled despite her reservations. "I suppose you're right."

"I usually am," Mrs. Jenkins replied with a wink. "Now, don't dawdle too long with that coffee."

After Mrs. Jenkins departed, Beth sipped the strong brew and contemplated her wardrobe. She'd planned to wear her light yellow dress for the picnic, but given the cooler, damp weather, she selected her blue dress instead. It was among the donated clothing, but Mrs. Turner had helped her take it in this past week and add modest embellishments that made it feel more her own.

As she dressed, Beth considered her growing attachment to Hopewell Creek and its people—particularly Ezra. Yet something held her back from fully embracing these feelings. Perhaps it was the memory of her failed journey to meet Henry Dobbins, or the knowledge that she still hadn't written to her parents since her terse departure note. Most concerning was the uncertain footing she still felt in this community, where she was establishing herself, but remained an outsider in many ways.

Beth fastened the last button on her dress, pushed these thoughts aside, and headed downstairs.

***

By eleven o'clock, the rain had dwindled to occasional drizzle, but gray clouds still blanketed the sky. Beth walked alongside Mrs. Jenkins toward the church, each carrying covered dishes for the social.

"I still don't understand why Maggie insisted I bring these rolls," Mrs. Jenkins grumbled good-naturedly. "Everyone knows her bread puts mine to shame."

"She said your dinner rolls were the only ones worthy of accompanying her ma's Irish stew," Beth reminded her, carefully balancing her potato salad.

"Flattery, pure and simple," Mrs. Jenkins sniffed, though she looked pleased.

As they approached the church, Beth noticed several wagons and buggies already parked outside. A flutter of anxiety tickled her stomach. Though she'd been in Hopewell Creek for two weeks, this would be her first major community gathering.

The community hall attached to the church bustled with activity. Long tables had been set up along the walls, already beginning to fill with an array of dishes. Children darted between adults, their energy undiminished by the weather. Women arranged flowers in mason jars, while men positioned additional benches and chairs.

Beth spotted Pastor Paul near the entrance, greeting arrivals.

"Mrs. Jenkins! Miss Beaumont! Wonderful to see you both," he called, his voice carrying over the din of conversation. "Please add your contributions to the bounty. We're blessed with abundance today."

They made their way to the food tables, where Maggie supervised the arrangement of dishes.

"There you are!" Maggie exclaimed, her red hair escaping its pins as usual. "Beth, that potato salad looks perfect. Put it right there between the pickles and ham."

Beth carefully set her dish down, removing the cloth covering. "I hope it's to everyone's liking. It's my mother's recipe."

"I'm sure it's wonderful," Maggie assured her. "Now, have you seen the dessert table? Sarah Collins brought her apple cobbler, and rumor has it Mrs. Simmons is sending her famous blackberry pie with Ezra."

At the mention of Ezra's name, Beth felt a warmth rise to her cheeks. "Is he here already?"

"Not yet," Maggie said, a knowing smile playing on her lips. "I'm sure he'll be along shortly."

Beth busied herself arranging napkins beside the plates, pretending not to notice Maggie's gentle teasing. She glanced around the room, taking in the familiar and not-so-familiar faces. The atmosphere was festive despite the dreary weather outside.

The door opened, bringing a gust of damp air and Ezra. His dark hair was slightly damp, and he carried a pie in one hand and a stack of newspapers under one arm. His eyes scanned the room, stopping when they found Beth. He smiled and made his way toward her.

"Beth," he greeted formally, though his eyes held warmth. "I thought people might appreciate some reading material if they're stuck indoors all afternoon. Extra editions from last week."

"That's thoughtful," Beth replied, conscious of Maggie watching their interaction with interest.

Ezra lowered his voice. "I hope you weren't disappointed about the change in the venue. I know you were looking forward to experiencing the picnic outdoors."

"There will be other opportunities," Beth said. "And the company matters more than the setting."

Ezra's smile deepened at her words, creating a small dimple in his right cheek that Beth hadn't noticed before.

The door swung open again, this time admitting Walter Fairfield and his daughter Rosalind. Rosalind wore a fashionable burgundy dress with more frills and lace than seemed practical for a community picnic. Her chestnut brown hair was arranged in an elaborate style that must have taken considerable time to achieve.

Rosalind's gaze swept the room imperiously before landing on Ezra and Beth. Her pleasant expression faltered momentarily before transforming into a brilliant smile as she steered her father in their direction.

"Ezra! How providential to find you so quickly," Rosalind called, her voice carrying across the hall. Several heads turned to watch her approach.

Ezra straightened, his smile becoming more reserved. "Miss Fairfield, Mr. Fairfield. Good afternoon."

"I was just telling Father how fortunate we are to have our newspaper editor so dedicated to community events," Rosalind said, placing her gloved hand on Ezra's arm. "You never miss an opportunity to chronicle our little town's activities, do you?"

"It's my job," Ezra replied simply, subtly shifting so that Rosalind's hand fell away. "And my pleasure."

Walter Fairfield nodded curtly toward Beth. "Miss Beaumont. Are you still settling in well at the Herald?"

"Yes, sir," Beth answered. "Mr. Simmons is most kind."

"Ezra has always had a gift for taking in strays," Rosalind remarked with a light laugh that didn't reach her eyes. "Such a compassionate nature."

Beth felt the sting of Rosalind's words. The implication was clear—Beth was a charity case, not a valued employee or community member.

"Miss Beaumont has a natural aptitude for newspaper work," Ezra countered firmly. "The Herald is fortunate to have found someone with her skills and intelligence, Rosalind."

Rosalind's smile tightened. "How fortunate indeed. And speaking of fortune, Ezra, I must tell you about the letter I received from my cousin in Denver. She's invited me to attend the summer concert series. Perhaps you'd be interested in accompanying me? Your cultural commentary would be so valuable to your readers."

Before Ezra could respond, Pastor Paul called for everyone's attention.

"Friends and neighbors, welcome to our spring social! Though the Lord has blessed our fields with much-needed rain today, He has also provided us with this wonderful hall to gather in fellowship. Let us bow our heads in thanksgiving before we enjoy the bounty before us."

As heads bowed, Beth glimpsed Rosalind watching her through barely lowered lashes. The young woman's expression was calculating, almost predatory. Beth quickly closed her eyes, but the unsettling feeling remained.

After the prayer, Pastor Paul directed everyone to form lines at the food tables. Beth became separated from Ezra as the crowd shifted. Rosalind, however, managed to maintain her position at his side, speaking animatedly into his ear.

Mrs. Jenkins appeared at Beth's elbow. "Don't let that girl bother you," she murmured. "Rosalind Fairfield has considered herself the queen of Hopewell Creek since she was in pigtails."

"She certainly seems... confident," Beth replied diplomatically.

"Hmph. That's one word for it. Another might be 'entitled.'" Mrs. Jenkins nudged Beth forward as the line moved. "Her father owns the bank as well as several other businesses, and her mother came from money in Boston. The Fairfields aren't used to hearing the word 'no.'"

Beth filled her plate with modest portions, conscious of Rosalind's eyes following her movements. When she reached her potato salad, she hesitated, suddenly self-conscious about her contribution.

"Is this your dish, dear?" Mrs. Turner asked, spooning a generous helping onto her plate. "It looks delicious."

"Yes, thank you," Beth replied.

"Such a simple offering," came Rosalind's voice from behind Mrs. Turner. "How... rustic. I suppose that's what one would expect from St. Louis cuisine."

Beth felt her cheeks warm. "It's a family recipe."

"Oh? I'd love to hear more about your family," Rosalind said, her tone suggesting idle curiosity, though her eyes were sharp. "You've mentioned so little about them since arriving in our community."

Several nearby conversations quieted as people turned to listen.

"There's not much to tell that would interest others," Beth said carefully.

"Now, don't be modest," Rosalind pressed. "A young woman travels all alone to Colorado—there must be quite a story there. Were your parents supportive of your... adventure?"

Beth felt trapped. The truth—that her parents had spiraled into addiction and debt after William's death, that she'd fled a desperate situation—wasn't something she wished to share with the entire community.

"My family circumstances are private, Miss Fairfield," Beth said with as much dignity as she could muster.

"Of course, of course," Rosalind replied with exaggerated understanding. "We all respect privacy. Though in small towns like ours, mysterious backgrounds do tend to spark curiosity."

Beth could feel curious glances from others in line. Rosalind had skillfully planted the seed of suspicion—what was Beth hiding?

"I find nothing mysterious about seeking honest work and a fresh start," came Ezra's voice as he appeared beside Beth, plate in hand. "It's the foundation of our western territories."

"How patriotic of you, Ezra," Rosalind said with a brittle smile. "Though, I believe a community thrives best when people are transparent about their intentions and history."

"A community thrives best when it practices Christian charity and welcomes strangers," Mrs. Jenkins interjected firmly. "As the Good Book says, 'Do not forget to show hospitality to strangers, for by so doing some people have shown hospitality to angels without knowing it.'"

Rosalind's smile remained fixed, but a flush crept up her neck. "I'm simply making conversation, Mrs. Jenkins. No need to deliver a sermon."

"Then perhaps we could converse about something more pleasant," Ezra suggested, guiding Beth toward a table where Maggie had saved seats. "The spring planting, perhaps, or the school's progress with their new scientific equipment."

Beth gratefully followed Ezra's lead, though she could feel Rosalind's gaze boring into her back. As they settled at the table with Maggie, Harriet, and Patrick O'Leary, Beth tried to shake off her discomfort.

"Don't mind Rosalind," Maggie whispered. "She's been eyeing Ezra like a prize heifer for years."

"Maggie," Patrick admonished, though his eyes twinkled with amusement.

"Well, it's true," Maggie insisted. "And she doesn't like competition, which is why she's sharpening her claws on Beth here."

"I'm not competition," Beth protested quietly. "Mr. Simmons is my employer and has been kind to me, that's all."

Maggie and Tom exchanged knowing glances, but said nothing more on the subject.

Conversation at their table turned to more pleasant topics—the recent success of Tom Bellwether's blacksmith business, the upcoming end-of-term program at the school, and a humorous story about Mrs. Jenkins' cat getting into the church choir robes.

Beth began to relax, laughing at Patrick's animated retelling of rescuing the cat from the rafters. She was so engaged in the conversation that she didn't immediately notice the subtle shift in the surrounding atmosphere. It was Ezra who first recognized the change, his expression growing concerned as he observed people at nearby tables.

Beth followed his gaze and saw two women whispering behind their hands, looking in her direction. At another table, a lady Beth didn't recognize was speaking in hushed tones to several ladies, who responded with raised eyebrows and sidelong glances at Beth.

"Is something wrong?" Beth asked quietly.

Ezra frowned. "I'm not sure. Excuse me for a moment."

He rose and approached Tom Bellwether, who was standing near the dessert table. They conversed briefly, with Tom looking uncomfortable and occasionally glancing toward Beth.

When Ezra returned to the table, his expression was troubled.

"What is it?" Beth asked, her stomach knotting with anxiety.

"It seems," Ezra said carefully, "that there are some... questions being raised about your arrival in Hopewell Creek."

"What kind of questions?" Beth's voice faltered.

Ezra hesitated, clearly reluctant to repeat what he'd heard.

"Rosalind is spreading rumors that you came here under false pretenses. That you're not being truthful about why you left St. Louis?"

Beth felt the blood drain from her face. "What exactly is she saying?"

"That perhaps you left St. Louis under some cloud of scandal," Ezra admitted reluctantly. "And that your interest in the newspaper—and in me—might be motivated by something other than honest work."

"That's absurd," Beth protested, though her mind raced. How much did Rosalind actually know about her circumstances?

"Of course it is," Maggie agreed firmly. "Anyone with sense can see you're an honest person."

"Unfortunately," Ezra said quietly, "small towns thrive on gossip, and Rosalind knows exactly which ears to whisper in."

Beth glanced around the room again, noticing how conversations seemed to halt momentarily when people caught her looking. Across the hall, Rosalind sat with her father and several prominent towns-people. She looked perfectly composed, occasionally glancing toward Beth with what appeared to be concern, though Beth recognized it as thinly veiled satisfaction.

"I should leave," Beth said, placing her napkin beside her half-eaten meal.

"That's precisely what she wants," Ezra replied, his voice low but intense. "If you leave now, it only gives credence to her insinuations."

"Ezra's right," Patrick agreed. "The Best way to face gossip is head-on."

Beth took a deep breath, trying to steady her nerves. "What should I do?"

"Act natural," Maggie advised. "Hold your head high. You've done nothing wrong."

"And let me handle Rosalind," Ezra added, his jaw set in determination.

Beth watched as Ezra stood and made his way toward Rosalind's table. His approach caused a momentary lull in their conversation.

Though Beth couldn't hear what was said, she could see the stiffness in Ezra's posture and the brief flash of surprise on Rosalind's face before she composed herself.

"What do you think he's saying to her?" Beth whispered to Maggie.

"Knowing Ezra? He's being perfectly polite while making it abundantly clear that spreading unfounded rumors reflects poorly on the rumormonger, not the subject." Maggie patted Beth's hand. "He may be a bookish fellow, but Ezra Simmons doesn't back down when something matters to him."

The thought that she might matter to Ezra brought both warmth and worry to Beth's heart. She didn't want to be the cause of conflict between him and the Fairfields, who clearly held significant influence in Hopewell Creek.

Beth forced herself to eat a few more bites of food, though it tasted like sawdust in her mouth. Around her, the atmosphere of the social continued, with people laughing and chatting, but she felt increasingly isolated, as though she existed in a bubble of suspicion.

Pastor Paul approached their table, his kind face creased with concern. "Miss Beaumont, I hope you're enjoying the gathering despite the weather."

"Yes, thank you, Pastor," Beth replied, mustering a smile.

"I wanted to thank you personally for your help with the church announcements in this week's paper. The clarity of your typesetting made even Brother Elijah's lengthy prayer meeting notice readable." His eyes twinkled with gentle humor.

Beth recognized his attempt to publicly demonstrate support and felt a rush of gratitude. "I'm still learning, but Mr. Simmons is an excellent teacher."

"Indeed, he is," Pastor Paul agreed. "Ezra has a gift for bringing out the best in people and situations. Much like his father." He raised his voice slightly, ensuring nearby tables could hear. "We're blessed to have you contributing to our community newspaper. The Herald has never looked better."

From the corner of her eye, Beth saw several people nodding in agreement, including Mrs. Turner, who had been whispering earlier. Perhaps not everyone was swayed by Rosalind's insinuations.

Ezra returned to their table, his expression more relaxed than when he'd left. "Pastor Paul, always a pleasure."

"I was just telling Miss Beaumont how much we appreciate the Herald's coverage of church events," Pastor Paul replied. "Will you be joining us for the hymn singing after the meal?"

"Wouldn't miss it," Ezra assured him.

As Pastor Paul moved on to greet the other tables, Ezra leaned closer to Beth. "Are you all right?"

"I think so," she replied, though her stomach remained in knots. "What did you say to Rosalind?"

"I simply reminded her that as a newspaper editor, I have a duty to report facts, not speculation. And that I take a dim view of anyone who would call into question the character of an honest, hardworking person without evidence."

Beth swallowed hard. "Thank you."

"There's nothing to thank me for," Ezra said firmly. "I would do the same for anyone unjustly maligned. The fact that it's you..." He hesitated, then continued more quietly, "Well, that only made it more important to speak up."

Their eyes met, and Beth felt that same connection she'd experienced during their buggy ride last Sunday. For a moment, the whispers and stares around them faded away.

Chapter 18

As Beth, Ezra, Harriet, and Patrick engaged in conversation, Mrs. Jenkins and Maggie arrived with a beautifully arranged tray of exquisite desserts.

"I'm not one for sweets usually, but Sarah's apple cobbler is not to be missed. And Beth, you must try a piece of Evelyn blackberry pie. It won the county fair three years running."

"Mother would be pleased to hear you recommending her pie so enthusiastically," Ezra said.

As they shared dessert, Beth began to feel the tension in her shoulders ease slightly. The conversations around them had resumed normal volume and topics, and fewer people seemed to be casting surreptitious glances her way.

After dessert, tables were pushed aside and chairs and benches arranged to create space for the hymn singing. Pastor Paul took his place at the small pump organ while his wife distributed hymnals.

"Let's sit near the front," Ezra suggested, guiding Beth forward. "Pastor Paul's enthusiasm for music sometimes outpaces his ability to stay on key, and it helps to have strong voices nearby."

Beth smiled at his gentle teasing of the pastor. As they found seats on a bench near the organ, she noticed several people nodding or smiling in greeting. Perhaps Ezra's public support and Pastor Paul's endorsement had helped stem the tide of gossip.

Rosalind and her father entered the singing area, Rosalind's eyes immediately finding Beth and Ezra. Her lips thinned when she saw them sitting together, but she quickly composed herself and led her father to seats directly behind them.

"Ezra," she called sweetly, "I brought you a hymnal. I know how you prefer the older edition with the traditional arrangements."

Before Ezra could respond, Mrs. Hawthorne handed Beth and Ezra each a hymnal. "Here you are, dears. We're starting with 'Blessed Assurance' today."

"Thank you, Mrs. Hawthorne," Ezra replied warmly.

As the music began, Beth found comfort in the familiar hymns. Her mother had often played these same songs on their piano in happier times. Beth's clear soprano blended well with Ezra's steady baritone, and for a few moments, she forgot her troubles in the harmony of congregational singing.

During a pause between hymns, Rosalind leaned forward, her voice pitched to carry just far enough for those nearby to hear. "Miss Beaumont, I couldn't help but notice your familiarity with the hymns. Were you active in a church in St. Louis? What was the name of your congregation? Perhaps someone here has connections there."

"We attended several churches over the years," Beth answered truthfully but vaguely.

"How unusual," Rosalind remarked. "Most families I know are quite dedicated to their home church. Unless, of course, there was some reason they needed to... move around."

The insinuation hung in the air, impossible to ignore.

"My father found spiritual nourishment in various Christian traditions," Beth said, thinking quickly. It wasn't entirely untrue—in better days, her father had enjoyed theological discussions with ministers of different denominations.

"How interesting," Rosalind said, her tone suggesting it was anything but. "And your mother shared this... denominational curiosity?"

Beth felt cornered, but before she could formulate a response, Ezra intervened.

"I find spiritual curiosity admirable," he said. "My own father reads widely across denominational lines. He says truth can be found in many pulpits if one listens with an open heart."

Several heads nodded in agreement, including Mrs. Hawthorne, who added, "Jacob Simmons is one of the wisest men in our community. If he endorses such an approach, there must be merit in it."

Rosalind's strategy had backfired, turning what was meant to be a pointed interrogation into a discussion of spiritual openness. Her smile became strained as she retreated.

"Of course," she murmured. "I simply find dedication to a single congregation builds stronger community bonds."

"There are many ways to build community," Pastor Paul said as he prepared for the next hymn. "Through music, through service, through honest work and friendship. Now, shall we continue with 'Rock of Ages'?"

As the singing resumed, Beth felt Ezra's hand briefly touch hers on the bench between them—a small gesture of reassurance. She didn't pull away, drawing strength from the connection.

The singing continued for another half hour before Pastor Paul concluded with a brief prayer of thanksgiving. As people began to disperse, some returning to the refreshment tables, while others prepared to brave the rain for home, Beth found herself surrounded by a small group, including Maggie, Mrs. Jenkins, and Mrs. Turner.

"Beth, I've been meaning to ask if you might help me with some delicate stitch work," Mrs. Turner said loudly enough for nearby conversations to pause. "I have a customer who wants elaborate embroidery on her daughter's wedding dress, and my eyes aren't what they used to be."

"I'd be happy to help," Beth replied, surprised by the sudden offer.

"Wonderful! I'll pay you fairly, of course."

"And you must share your potato salad recipe," Maggie added. "Father hasn't stopped talking about it today."

Beth realized they were publicly aligning themselves with her, countering Rosalind's attempts to isolate her socially. Gratitude warmed her chest.

"I'd be delighted to share the recipe," she said. "Though I warn you, the secret is patience. You make it the day before serving to let the flavors come alive."

"Patience... something Miss Fairfield could learn from," Mrs. Jenkins muttered, just loud enough for their circle to hear.

Beth suppressed a laugh, glancing across the room where Rosalind stood with her father, clearly displeased by the show of support for Beth.

As the social wound down, Beth helped with cleaning up, washing dishes alongside other women in the church kitchen. The familiar domestic task soothed her nerves, and she engaged in easy conversation about recipes and household tips—normal, everyday exchanges that made her feel more accepted.

When the last dish was dried and put away, Beth found her shawl and prepared to leave. The rain had stopped, though puddles dotted the muddy street and the air remained heavy with moisture.

"May I walk you back to Mrs. Jenkins?" Ezra asked, appearing at her side.

"Thank you, but I really don't want to be of any trouble," Beth replied, mindful of how their growing closeness had already fueled Rosalind's jealousy.

"It's no trouble," Ezra insisted.

Beth nodded, and they stepped outside into the damp evening air, the sky beginning to clear as sunset approached.

"I'm sorry about what happened today. Rosalind was out of line," Ezra said.

"It's not your fault," Beth said. "And to be fair, my arrival in Hopewell Creek was unusual. It's natural for people to be curious."

"Curiosity is one thing. Malicious gossip is another." Ezra's voice hardened. "Rosalind deliberately tried to undermine your position here."

Beth sighed. "Because she sees me as a threat to her... expectations regarding you."

Ezra looked uncomfortable. "Rosalind has certain assumptions that I've never encouraged. Unfortunately, her father is an influential man in town, and I've tried to maintain cordial relations."

"I understand," Beth said quickly. "You don't owe me any explanation."

"Perhaps not," Ezra conceded. "But I want you to know that I value your presence in Hopewell Creek—at the newspaper and... elsewhere."

The hesitation in his voice made Beth glance up at him. His expression was earnest, his eyes searching hers.

"That means a great deal to me," she said.

They turned onto the street where Mrs. Jenkins' boarding house stood, its windows glowing with welcoming lamplight. Beth's steps slowed, reluctant to end their conversation despite her earlier resolution to maintain professional distance.

"Beth," Ezra said, using her given name with careful deliberation, "I hope today's events won't make you withdraw from community gatherings. Your presence enriches our town."

Beth considered his words. Part of her wanted to retreat, to protect herself from further scrutiny and gossip. It would be easier to focus solely on her work, to avoid social entanglements that might lead to more painful confrontations like today's.

"I won't withdraw," she said finally. "But I think I need to be cautious. My position here is still... precarious."

Ezra nodded slowly. "I understand. But please remember you're not alone here. You have allies—more than you might realize."

They reached the gate of Mrs. Jenkins' yard. In the fading light, Beth could see the genuine concern in Ezra's expression, and it touched something deep within her. Despite her resolve to guard her heart, she couldn't deny the growing connection between them.

"Thank you for defending me today," she said. "It would have been easier for you to stay neutral."

"Easier, perhaps, but not right," Ezra replied simply. "My father taught me that character reveals itself most clearly when standing up for others comes at a personal cost."

The wisdom in his words reminded Beth of her own father. A pang of homesickness struck her unexpectedly.

"Your parents raised a good man," she said quietly.

Ezra smiled, the expression softening his features. "I'll see you at church tomorrow?"

"Of course," Beth confirmed.

"May I come and walk with you again?"

"Yes, you may. Goodnight, Ezra."

He nodded and smiled before he turned to walk home.

She watched him walk away, his figure gradually blending into the gathering darkness. Only when he turned the corner did she open the gate and make her way to the boarding house door.

Chapter 19

Mrs. Jenkins sat in the parlor with her knitting. She looked up as Beth entered, assessing her with keen eyes.

"You handled yourself well today," she said without preamble. "Not everyone would have maintained such dignity in the face of Rosalind Fairfield's tactics."

"I nearly fled," Beth admitted, sinking into a chair opposite the older woman.

"But you didn't," Mrs. Jenkins pointed out, her needles clicking steadily. "That's what matters."

Beth stared into the small fire burning in the grate. "I'm not sure if I belong here, Mrs. Jenkins. Perhaps coming to Hopewell Creek was a mistake."

The knitting needles paused. "And where do you think you belong, child?"

The question caught Beth off guard. Not St. Louis, certainly—not with the painful memories and her parents' deterioration. Where did she belong?

"I don't know," she confessed.

Mrs. Jenkins resumed her knitting. "Then this is as good a place as any to find out. Better than most, I'd say."

"Even with Rosalind working against me?"

"Especially then," Mrs. Jenkins said firmly. "Challenges reveal our true mettle. And they help us recognize our true friends."

Beth thought of Ezra, of Maggie and the O'Leary's, of Pastor Paul and his wife—all who had shown her kindness and support.

"I suppose you're right," she conceded.

"I usually am," Mrs. Jenkins replied, echoing her words from the morning with a small smile. "Now, you should rest. Tomorrow will bring its own concerns, as the Good Book says."

Beth excused herself and climbed the stairs to her room, her mind still processing the day's events. Once inside, she lit the lamp and moved to the window, gazing out at the now-clear night sky where stars had begun to appear.

The day had been difficult, revealing the fragility of her position in Hopewell Creek. Rosalind's antagonism had shaken her more than she wanted to admit. Yet, it had also shown her the strength of new friendships forming and, perhaps most surprisingly, Ezra's willingness to stand beside her publicly.

Beth opened her trunk and withdrew her Bible. She turned to Isaiah, the passage that had given her courage on the train: "I will make a way in the wilderness and rivers in the desert."

Her situation remained precarious. Her heart, despite her best efforts, was becoming entangled with Ezra. And now Rosalind Fairfield had declared a subtle war against her.

The safest path would be to guard her heart, to focus solely on establishing her independence. Love had brought her mother nothing but pain in the end. Community acceptance, as today had proven, was fragile and conditional.

Yet as Beth closed her Bible and prepared for bed, a small, resilient part of her refused to surrender hope completely. Despite her resolution to protect herself from vulnerability, the memory of Ezra's steadfast defense warmed her. Perhaps there was still a way forward in this wilderness, if she had the courage to continue.

Beth kneeled beside the bed and folded her hands, bowing her head as she had done since childhood. For a moment, she hesitated, uncertain of what to pray. Then she began to speak softly, her voice gaining strength as she continued.

"Heavenly Father, I come to You tonight with a heart full of uncertainty. This path You've set before me is not the one I expected, and I confess I'm afraid. Please grant me the wisdom to know Your will and the courage to follow it, even when the way seems unclear."

"Lord, I ask for Your guidance as I build this new life in Hopewell Creek. Help me to conduct myself with honor and integrity, even when faced with those who doubt me. Give me strength to weather the storms of gossip and suspicion with the same grace that Your Son showed in the face of His accusers."

"I pray especially for my parents tonight. Though I left them in anger and disappointment, my heart aches for them still. Please comfort them in my absence, and if it be Your will, lead them back to the path of righteousness. Help them find their way back to You, Lord, as they once knew You. May they find healing from the grief that has consumed them since William's passing."

"Watch over me in the days ahead, Father. Guard my heart and my steps. When I am weak, be my strength. When I am lost, be my compass. And when I am tempted to doubt Your plan for me, remind me of Your faithfulness through all generations."

"In Jesus' name, I pray. Amen."

Chapter 20

Beth hurried along Main Street toward the Herald office, her steps light despite the early hour. The morning air felt crisp against her cheeks, carrying the promise of another warm late spring day. She'd left the boarding house earlier than necessary, eager to begin the week's work.

Her mind drifted to Ezra's promise to teach her about advertising layouts today. In just over two weeks, she'd gone from stranded stranger to newspaper assistant with growing confidence in her abilities. The thought brought a smile to her lips as she rounded the corner toward the Herald.

The smile vanished as a figure emerged from the shadowed space between buildings. Beth's steps faltered as recognition hit her like a physical blow.

Henry Dobbins.

He leaned against the wall, disheveled and unsteady. His shirt was wrinkled and stained, his eyes bloodshot, and stubble darkened his jaw. When he spotted her, a slow, unpleasant smile spread across his face.

"Well, if it ain't Miss Beaumont," he slurred, pushing himself off the wall.

Beth's throat constricted. She glanced around, noting with dismay that the street was nearly empty at this early hour. The Herald's windows showed lamplight inside—Ezra was already working—but it lay twenty paces ahead.

"Mr. Dobbins," she acknowledged stiffly, lifting her chin. "Please excuse me. I'm expected at work."

She attempted to walk past him, but he stepped directly into her path.

"Not so fast." His breath reeked of whiskey. "Seems we got business to discuss, you and me."

"We have no business whatsoever," Beth replied, fighting to keep her voice steady. "Please step aside."

Henry's expression darkened. "That ain't no way to talk, considering your situation." He swayed slightly. "Wife's gone. Packed up and left three days ago. Said she was tired of my schemes."

Beth took a step back. "I'm sorry to hear that, but it doesn't concern me."

"Oh, but it does." Henry followed, closing the distance between them. "See, I got to thinking. You came all this way to be a bride. I find myself in need of a wife." His smile turned predatory. "Seems like a solution for both of us."

Beth felt sick. "You cannot be serious."

"Dead serious." Henry's tone hardened. "You ain't exactly swimming in options. Working at that newspaper, living on charity. What kind of life is that?"

"A far better one than anything you could offer," Beth said, her voice stronger now.

Henry's face contorted with anger. He lunged forward, grabbing Beth's arm. His fingers dug painfully into her flesh.

"Listen here," he hissed. "You think these people respect you? You think they'd still smile so nice if they knew the truth? That you came running halfway across the country to marry a man you'd never even exchanged a letter with?" His grip tightened. "How desperate does a woman have to be to do something like that? What kind of woman just up and leaves everything behind without so much as—"

"Let go of her."

Ezra's voice cut through Henry's tirade like a blade. Beth hadn't seen him emerge from the Herald, but now he stood just feet away, his normally gentle face set in hard lines.

Henry didn't release Beth's arm. "This ain't your concern, news-paperman. This is between me and—"

"I said, let go of her." Ezra's voice remained level, but there was steel beneath the words. His eyes flicked briefly to Beth's face, reading her distress.

Henry sneered. "You defending her honor? You know what kind of woman she is? Running off to marry a stranger—"

In two swift strides, Ezra closed the distance between them. With one hand, he gripped Henry's wrist and squeezed until Henry's fingers released Beth's arm. With his other hand, Ezra gently moved Beth behind him.

"Miss Beaumont is my employee and friend," Ezra said, his voice dangerously quiet. "And you're drunk before eight in the morning, assaulting a woman on a public street."

Henry tried to pull his wrist free, but Ezra's grip remained firm.

"I suggest you leave. Now. And don't approach Miss Beaumont again." Ezra released Henry's wrist with a slight push that sent the drunken man stumbling back a step.

Henry rubbed his wrist, his bloodshot eyes darting between Ezra and Beth. "This ain't over."

"Yes, it is," Ezra replied evenly. "Sheriff Miller would be mighty interested to hear about your mail-order bride scheme. I imagine there are laws against such fraud."

Henry's face paled slightly beneath its stubble. "You wouldn't have proof."

"The other women who arrived in Hopewell Creek under false pretenses, plus Beth herself, might disagree. Not to mention your own wife." Ezra crossed his arms. "Walk away, Dobbins. Leave town if you're smart."

For a tense moment, Henry looked like he might lunge at Ezra. Then he spat on the ground between them.

"You're welcome to her," he snarled. "Desperate woman like that—probably hiding worse than she's telling."

Ezra took a step forward, and Henry hastily retreated.

"This ain't the last you'll hear from me," Henry called as he backed away. "Either of you."

They watched in silence as Henry staggered down the street, disappearing around a corner.

Ezra turned to Beth, concern replacing the anger on his face. "Are you hurt?"

Beth realized she was trembling. "No, I—" Her voice caught.

"Come inside," Ezra said gently. He placed a careful hand at her elbow, guiding her toward the Herald office.

Once inside, Ezra locked the door behind them and flipped the sign to "Closed." Without a word, he pulled a chair out for Beth. As she sank into it, the full impact of the encounter hit her. Her legs felt suddenly unable to support her weight.

Ezra moved to his desk, pulled out a flask, and poured the liquid into a cup.

"Just water," he explained, handing it to her.

Beth accepted the cup gratefully, taking a sip.

"Thank you," she said. "I'm sorry to cause such trouble."

"You've caused nothing," Ezra said firmly, pulling another chair to sit across from her. "Dobbins is the only one at fault here." He hesitated. "Has he approached you before this?"

Beth shook her head. "Not since that first day." She stared down at her cup. "I never thought he'd... that he would suggest..."

"You don't need to speak of it," Ezra assured her.

"But I do." Beth looked up, meeting his eyes. "I need to tell you everything, Ezra. About St. Louis. About why I came here. If Rosalind starts spreading more rumors, or if Henry tells people what he threatened to tell..."

Ezra's expression softened. "Beth, you don't owe me or anyone else explanations about your past."

"Perhaps not. But I want you to know the truth." She took a deep breath. "I haven't told anyone about all of my reasons for coming to Hopewell Creek."

Beth placed her cup on the desk and continued. "My family in St. Louis... they weren't just 'lost,' as I've sometimes implied. After my brother William died, my parents changed. Father turned to gambling and drink to numb his grief. Mother began drinking as well."

The memories rose like ghosts, painful and persistent. "They had once been devoted Christians. Good society people. But grief twisted them into strangers. Father lost his position as an accountant. Eventually, we moved to increasingly shabby accommodations as debts mounted. The drinking worsened. The fights became..." She swallowed hard. "Frightening."

Ezra's face remained compassionate, without judgment.

"I tried to help. I mended clothes for neighbors, took in washing when I could. But it was never enough." Beth clasped her hands together to still their trembling. "The day I left, our landlord had threatened eviction. Father was gone again. Mother was..." She couldn't finish.

"That day, I saw Henry's advertisement in a newspaper. A God-fearing man in Colorado seeking a Christian wife." Beth's laugh held no humor. "It seemed like divine intervention—a sign pointing to escape. I didn't think it through. I simply packed my trunk, wrote a brief note to my parents, and left."

She looked up at Ezra, waiting for the disapproval or shock that must surely come. "I never corresponded with Henry. I sent one letter announcing my departure the day I boarded the train, but it couldn't have arrived before I did. I was desperate and foolish, and I placed my trust in a stranger's advertisement."

To her surprise, Ezra's expression remained unchanged. "You were trapped in an impossible situation and found the courage to leave," he said quietly. "There's nothing shameful about that."

"But to come as a mail-order bride to a man I'd never met or corresponded with—"

"You sought a better life, Beth. A chance to rebuild what you'd lost." Ezra leaned forward slightly. "The shame belongs to Henry Dobbins for preying on women in difficult circumstances, not to those women for seeking escape."

Beth felt tears threatening. "Henry's right, though. What will people think when they learn the truth? That I was so desperate to flee my home that I responded to an advertisement without even exchanging letters first?"

"They'll see a young woman of remarkable courage," Ezra replied without hesitation. "Someone who faced terrible circumstances and chose to seek something better rather than surrender to despair."

His certainty made her want to believe him. "You're very kind."

"It's no kindness to see what's plainly before me." Ezra's voice grew softer. "From the moment you arrived in Hopewell Creek, you've shown nothing but dignity, hard work, and grace—despite having every reason to be bitter or defeated."

Beth wiped at an escaped tear. "I don't feel particularly dignified or graceful most days."

"That only makes your strength more remarkable." Ezra hesitated, then continued, "My mother always says that courage isn't about feeling brave. It's about being afraid and moving forward, anyway. I believe that."

"Your mother is such a wise woman."

"She is." His smile held both sadness and fondness. "She likes you very much."

The simple statement warmed Beth more than she could express.

Ezra rose and moved to the stove in the corner of the office. "I think we both could use some coffee after that ordeal."

As he busied himself with the coffeepot, Beth gathered her composure. The panic from Henry's appearance had receded, but his words still echoed in her mind. Would the people of Hopewell Creek truly understand if they knew her full story?

"Ezra," she said suddenly, "I think I should leave Hopewell Creek."

He turned sharply, coffeepot in hand. "What?"

"Henry's threat to tell everyone about how I came here—it would cause embarrassment for you and the Herald." She twisted her hands in her lap. "Mrs. Jenkins has been so kind, and Pastor Paul and his wife... I couldn't bear to bring scandal to—"

"Beth." Ezra set down the coffeepot and returned to his chair. "There will be no scandal. Henry Dobbins is a known liar and drunkard. No one of consequence would believe anything he says."

"Rosalind would."

"Rosalind looks for reasons to find fault," Ezra said dismissively. "That reflects on her character, not yours."

Beth wasn't convinced. "Even so—"

"Even so, nothing." Ezra's voice was firm. "You belong here, Beth. You've earned your place in Hopewell Creek through honest work and genuine goodness. I won't hear of you leaving because of Henry Dobbins's threats or Rosalind Fairfield's jealousy."

The word "jealousy," caught Beth by surprise. "Jealousy? Why would Rosalind be jealous of me?"

Ezra's ears reddened slightly. "Well, because..." He cleared his throat. "She's developed certain... expectations regarding our relationship that I've never encouraged. Your arrival and our friendship have disrupted those expectations."

Beth felt a flutter in her chest that had nothing to do with fear.

Ezra turned back to the stove, his movements slightly more hurried than necessary. "In any case, you needn't worry about town opinion. Hopewell Creek values hard work and character far more than pristine backgrounds. Half the town came here running from something."

He returned with two steaming cups of coffee. "Including my own father, though he doesn't speak of it often."

Beth accepted the coffee gratefully. "Your father? What was he running from?"

"Deceitful parents. His parents had been high society and very prestigious people in Philadelphia. His parents lost everything because they were embezzling funds. They tried throwing much of the blame on my father." Ezra settled into his chair. "He was courting my mother at the time. They married quickly, and came west with nothing but a wagon of belongings and a determination to start fresh."

"I had no idea," Beth said softly.

"Few do. It's not a secret, but it's not something he discusses frequently." Ezra sipped his coffee. "The point is, most people here understand that second chances are the very foundation of places like Hopewell Creek."

Beth found herself smiling despite the tumultuous morning.

Ezra's smile matched hers. "I intend to speak with Sheriff Miller about Mr. Dobbins, nonetheless. His behavior this morning crossed a line."

The reminder of Henry's proposition made Beth shudder involuntarily. "Do you think he'll truly leave town?"

"Hard to say." Ezra's expression grew serious. "But until we're certain, I'd prefer you not walk alone, especially in the early morning or evening."

Under normal circumstances, Beth might have bristled at the suggestion that she needed protection. But the memory of Henry's grip on her arm was too fresh. "That seems wise."

"I can escort you to and from the boarding house," Ezra offered. "And I'm sure Maggie or Mrs. Jenkins would accompany you at other times if needed."

"Thank you." Beth took another sip of coffee, letting its warmth soothe her. "For defending me against Henry. For listening without judgment."

"You needn't thank me for basic decency," Ezra said.

"It hasn't always been basic in my experience," Beth replied.

Something in her tone made Ezra study her face more intently. "Beth, when you spoke of your parents' fights becoming frightening... were you ever in danger?"

The question hung between them, more perceptive than she'd expected. Beth stared into her coffee cup, debating how much to reveal.

"Not physically," she said finally. "At least, not intentionally. But when Father was in a rage about gambling losses, or Mother was in one of her deep drinking states, objects were thrown. Furniture overturned." She swallowed hard. "Once, Father swept everything from the mantelpiece in a fit of anger. A heavy brass candlestick nearly struck me."

Ezra's expression darkened.

"He was horrified afterward," Beth added quickly. "He wept and apologized for days. But it was... difficult to feel safe after that."

"I can imagine." Ezra's voice was gentle, but held an undercurrent of controlled anger. "No one should have to live with such uncertainty."

"No," Beth agreed softly. "They weren't always that way. Before William died, our home was peaceful. Orderly. It was a home filled with love and faith. Father read Scripture each evening. Mother sang hymns while she worked." The contrast between then and now struck her anew. "I still find it hard to understand how grief could transform them so completely."

"Grief affects people differently," Ezra said. "After Ellen died, my mother withdrew completely. For months, she barely spoke or left her room. Father threw himself into ranch work, exhausting himself daily so he could sleep at night."

Beth nodded. "You mentioned that before."

"What I didn't mention was my own response." Ezra's gaze drifted to the window. "I became angry. At God, at the doctor who couldn't save her, at my parents for their own grieving." His voice quieted. "I even felt angry at Ellen sometimes, for leaving us."

The confession clearly cost him. Beth reached across the desk and touched his hand lightly. "You were young."

"Sixteen. Old enough to know better." He shook his head. "I picked fights at school. Stopped attending church. Started spending time with boys my father disapproved of."

Beth tried to reconcile this image with the steady, principled man before her. "What changed?"

"Pastor Paul, actually." A faint smile touched Ezra's lips. "He found me behind the livery one day, bloodied from a fight. Instead of lecturing me, he simply said, 'When you're ready to talk about Ellen, I'll listen.' Then he helped clean me up and walked me home."

Ezra shifted in his chair. "A week later, I found myself at his door. We talked for hours—about Ellen, about grief, about anger. He didn't offer easy answers or platitudes. He just listened."

"How truly kind of him," Beth said softly.

"It was the beginning of finding my way back." Ezra met her eyes again. "What I'm trying to say is that I understand something of how grief can alter a person. Your parents' response was particularly destructive, but the root—that overwhelming pain—is something I recognize."

Beth felt tears threatening again. No one had ever spoken about her parents with such compassion before.

"I've prayed for them," she admitted. "Even after everything. Is that foolish?"

"Not at all." Ezra's voice was warm. "Prayer is never wasted, even when we can't see its effects."

For a long moment, they sat in companionable silence, the morning's trauma softened by shared understanding.

"We should probably open the office," Beth said eventually, glancing at the clock.

"In a bit," Ezra replied. "First, I need to speak with Sheriff Miller about Henry. Would you be comfortable accompanying me, or would you prefer to stay here?"

Beth considered. The thought of recounting the morning's events was unpleasant, but the alternative—waiting alone in the office—seemed worse.

"I'll come with you," she decided. "If Sheriff Miller is to understand the situation fully, he should hear from both of us."

Ezra nodded approvingly. "That's my thinking as well."

They finished their coffee and prepared to leave. As Ezra held the door for her, Beth paused.

"Ezra," she said quietly, "when you spoke to Henry—when you called me your friend—did you mean it?"

His expression softened. "Of course I did. I consider you a very dear friend, Beth."

Something in his tone suggested a deeper meaning, but Beth didn't dare interpret it.

"I feel the same," she said simply.

Chapter 21

Sheriff Jonas Miller's office sat halfway down Main Street, a tidy building with "Sheriff" painted in black letters on the front window. As they approached, Ezra subtly shortened his stride to match Beth's, a small courtesy that didn't escape her notice.

The sheriff was at his desk when they entered, writing in a ledger. He looked up, his rugged face breaking into a smile.

"Mr. Simmons, Miss Beaumont. What brings you to my humble establishment this morning?"

Ezra removed his hat. "We need to report an incident, Sheriff."

Miller's expression immediately turned serious. He gestured to the chairs before his desk. "Have a seat and tell me what happened."

As they settled into the chairs, Beth suddenly felt hesitant. Speaking about the confrontation meant reliving it, and some part of her worried that the sheriff might view her actions—coming to Hopewell Creek as she had—with disapproval.

Ezra seemed to sense her discomfort. "Sheriff, Miss Beaumont was accosted by Henry Dobbins this morning outside the Herald office," he began. "He was intoxicated and became physically aggressive."

Sheriff Miller's gaze sharpened as it moved to Beth. "Is that so, Miss Beaumont?"

Beth nodded, finding her voice. "Yes. He...he grabbed my arm quite forcefully and made inappropriate suggestions."

The sheriff reached for a pencil. "I'll need the details, if you're able to provide them."

Drawing a steadying breath, Beth recounted the morning's events—from Henry's initial appearance to his proposition and threats. She omitted only the most personal aspects of her background, focusing instead on Henry's behavior and menacing manner.

"Mr. Simmons intervened," she concluded. "I dread to think what might have happened otherwise."

Sheriff Miller made notes throughout her account. When she finished, he turned to Ezra. "Anything to add, Mr. Simmons?"

"Only that Dobbins explicitly threatened both of us before leaving," Ezra replied. "He said, 'This ain't the last you'll hear from me.'"

The sheriff nodded grimly. "I've had my eye on Dobbins for some time. Between his mail-order bride schemes and his drinking, he's been a nuisance to this town. I suspect he's also swindled money from several women who came this way, thinking they were to marry him. A few of the women who arrived... disappeared without a trace, but I have no solid evidence of all this, hearsay, is all it is." He set down his pencil. "I'll have a talk with him today. Make it clear that any further harassment will result in his arrest."

"I appreciate that, Sheriff," Beth said.

"In the meantime," Miller continued, "I suggest you avoid being alone, particularly in the early morning or evening. Drink can change a man's nature, and Dobbins does plenty of it."

"I've already offered to escort Miss Beaumont to and from the boarding house," Ezra said.

Sheriff Miller nodded approvingly. "Good. And Miss Beaumont, should Dobbins approach you again—at any time, for any reason—I want to know about it immediately."

"Yes, Sheriff."

Miller closed his ledger. "Now, there's one more matter we should discuss." His gaze was direct, but not unkind. "Dobbins threatened to spread talk about your arrival in Hopewell Creek."

Beth tensed. "Yes."

"I don't pry into folks' pasts as a rule," the sheriff said carefully. "But if there's anything I should know—anything that might affect how I handle this situation—now would be the time to share it."

Beth glanced at Ezra, who gave her an encouraging nod.

"I came to Hopewell Creek in response to Mr. Dobbins's advertisement for a mail-order bride," she said plainly. "I had never corresponded with him. I simply saw the advertisement, made a hasty decision to leave St. Louis, and arrived to discover he was already married."

She lifted her chin slightly. "I left a difficult family situation in St. Louis. My parents had fallen into gambling and drinking after my brother's death. I sought escape and a fresh start. I have done nothing illegal. I chose to leave a bad situation in hopes of something better for myself. My only sin is walking away from my parents, who desperately needed help."

Sheriff Miller's expression remained neutral. "I see. I wouldn't consider walking away from a terrible situation a sin, Ms. Beaumont. Have you had any contact with your family since leaving?"

"No, sir," Beth replied. "I left a note explaining I was heading west, but provided no specifics."

"They haven't attempted to locate you?"

"I very much doubt they've tried." The admission hurt, despite everything. "They were... consumed by their own troubles. I highly doubt they will ever search for me."

The sheriff nodded, seemingly satisfied. "Thank you for your honesty, Miss Beaumont. It helps me understand the full picture." He leaned back in his chair. "For what it's worth, you wouldn't be the first person to come to Hopewell Creek seeking a fresh start. Half this town, myself included, came west running from something."

The echo of Ezra's earlier words made Beth smile slightly. "So I've been told."

Sheriff Miller rose, signaling the end of their meeting. "I'll speak with Dobbins today. In the meantime, stay vigilant, and don't hesitate to call on me if you have any concerns."

As they left the sheriff's office, Beth felt strangely lightened. The secret she had carried—the fear of judgment for her impulsive journey west—seemed less burdensome now that it had been spoken aloud to both Ezra and Sheriff Miller.

"Are you alright?" Ezra asked as they walked back toward the Herald.

"Better than I expected to be," Beth admitted. "Sheriff Miller was very understanding."

"Jonas is a good man. Practical and fair-minded." Ezra glanced down at her. "I apologize for not telling you more about Henry... more about what some suspect him of. I should have been more vigilant and escorted you everywhere. I didn't think he'd approach you directly."

"You couldn't have known, and you intervened when it mattered most," Beth assured him. "What happens now?"

"Now," Ezra said with a small smile, "we return to work. I believe I promised to teach you about advertising layouts today."

Beth smiled back, grateful for the return to normalcy. "So you did."

"And this evening," Ezra continued, "if you feel up to it, I thought we might take supper at the café."

The simple invitation lifted Beth's spirits. "That sounds lovely."

Chapter 22

"Good afternoon!" Maggie called cheerfully, stepping inside the Herald with a basket over her arm. "Mother sent lunch for both of you. She's testing a new soup recipe and wants honest opinions."

"How fortunate for us," Ezra said with a grin. "Mrs. O'Leary's experiments are always delicious."

Maggie set the basket on Beth's desk and began unpacking it. "Potato soup, fresh bread, and apple tarts." She looked up at Beth. "Mother says you're looking too thin and need feeding up."

Beth laughed. "Please thank her for the kind concern."

"Have you heard about Henry Dobbins?" Maggie asked.

Beth and Ezra exchanged glances.

"What about him?" Ezra asked carefully.

"Sheriff Miller escorted him to the edge of town about an hour ago," Maggie reported. "Told him not to return unless he wanted to spend time in a cell. Father saw it happen from the store window."

Relief washed over Beth. "He's gone?"

"Apparently so. Good riddance, I say." Maggie's normally cheerful face darkened. "After what he did to those other women... and to you, Beth."

"You know about that?" Beth asked, surprised.

Maggie nodded. "Mother told me how you arrived. She doesn't like gossip, mind you, but she thought I should know, so I wouldn't accidentally say something hurtful."

The consideration behind this revelation touched Beth deeply.

"I hope you don't mind," Maggie continued, suddenly uncertain. "Mother and I, we just want you to feel welcome here."

"I don't mind at all," Beth assured her. "And I do feel welcome. Thanks in large part to you and your family."

Maggie beamed. "Good! Now, eat your soup before it gets cold. Mother will quiz me on your reactions."

They enjoyed the hearty soup and fresh bread while Maggie entertained them with stories from the café.

When Maggie departed, promising to save them seats at the café for supper, Beth felt considerably lighter in spirit.

"Maggie is a treasure," she remarked as she and Ezra cleared away the remains of lunch.

"That she is," Ezra agreed. "Hopewell Creek would be a duller place without the O'Learys."

They returned to their work, the afternoon passing in comfortable productivity. Beth finished organizing the announcements and moved on to proofreading several articles Ezra had prepared for the upcoming edition.

At four o'clock, Ezra stretched and set down his pen. "I think that's enough for today. The editorial is finished, and you've made excellent progress on the announcements."

Beth looked up from her desk. "Are you certain? I'm happy to continue if there's more to be done."

"There's always more to be done at a newspaper," Ezra said with a smile. "But it will keep until tomorrow." He hesitated. "If you'd like, we could take a walk before supper. The afternoon is pleasant, and some fresh air might be welcome after being indoors all day."

The invitation pleased her, though a small voice of caution whispered that she was growing too fond of these moments with Ezra.

"I'd like that very much," she replied, setting those concerns aside. After the morning's events, she deserved this small happiness.

They left the Herald office together, turning toward the west end of town. The late afternoon sun cast a golden light over the buildings, and a gentle breeze carried the scent of pine from the surrounding hills.

"I was thinking we might walk to the creek," Ezra suggested. "It's particularly peaceful this time of day."

Beth nodded her agreement, remembering their previous visit to the stream that gave the town its name.

As they walked, Ezra kept a respectful distance beside her, though close enough that his presence felt protective rather than formal. They passed several townspeople who greeted them warmly, with no hint of the judgment Beth had feared after Henry's threats.

"Sheriff Miller works quickly," Ezra remarked as they left the last buildings behind. "I'm relieved that Dobbins has been sent on his way."

"As am I," Beth admitted. "Though I wonder if he'll truly stay away."

"If he returns, he'll face immediate arrest," Ezra assured her. "Jonas Miller doesn't make idle threats."

The path to the creek wound through a small grove of cottonwood trees, their leaves rustling softly in the breeze. As they emerged from the trees, the creek came into view—a ribbon of clear water flowing over smooth stones, with wildflowers dotting its banks.

They found a fallen log near the water's edge and sat down. For a while, they simply enjoyed the peaceful sounds of the creek and birdsong.

"I've been thinking," Ezra said eventually, "about what you said this morning—about believing God guided you to Hopewell Creek."

Beth glanced at him. "Yes?"

"I believe you're right." His gaze remained on the flowing water. "When Marjorie left the newspaper, I worried about finding someone suitable to replace her. Someone with intelligence, diligence, and integrity."

He turned to face her. "Then you arrived, under the most unlikely circumstances. It seemed... providential."

The earnestness in his expression made Beth's heart beat faster. "Do you truly think so?"

"I do." Ezra's voice was quiet but certain. "Beth, I—"

He paused, seeming to search for words. The intensity of his gaze made Beth acutely aware of how close they sat on the log.

"I want you to know," he continued carefully, "that regardless of how you came to Hopewell Creek, I'm grateful you're here. Not just because you're an excellent assistant, but because..."

Beth held her breath.

"Because knowing you has been a blessing," he finished. "Your courage, your kindness, your faith despite adversity—they remind me daily of what truly matters."

The words touched Beth deeply. "I feel the same about knowing you."

Ezra's expression shifted—a softening, a certainty. Slowly, telegraphing his intent, he reached for her hand.

Beth met him halfway, her fingers slipping into his. The simple touch felt momentous, like crossing a threshold into something new and precious.

"I want to be completely honest with you," Ezra said, his voice low. "My feelings for you have grown beyond friendship. I care for you deeply, Beth."

The confession both thrilled and frightened her. "Ezra, I—" She swallowed, gathering courage. "I care for you, too. Very much."

"I don't want to rush you. I know you've experienced much uncertainty lately. But I want you to know that my intentions are honorable, and when you're ready—"

A sharp crack of breaking branches interrupted him. Beth turned toward the sound, expecting to see a deer, or perhaps children, from town playing near the creek.

Instead, Henry Dobbins sat astride a weathered dun horse at the edge of the trees, his face contorted with fury. His clothes were rumpled, his eyes bloodshot, and he swayed slightly in the saddle.

"Well, ain't this sweet," he sneered, his words slurring. "The newspaper man and his charity case."

Ezra stood immediately, positioning himself between Beth and Henry. "You were warned to leave town, Dobbins. Sheriff Miller will—"

"Sheriff Miller ain't nothin'," Henry spat. His gaze shifted to Beth, his eyes narrowing. "This is your fault. All of it."

Beth rose to her feet, her heart pounding. "Mr. Dobbins, please. No one intended—"

"Shut your mouth!" Henry's face darkened with rage. "You brought this on me. Coming here with your pathetic dreams, thinking you deserve better than what you are."

Ezra took a step forward, his voice steady but firm. "That's enough, Dobbins. You need to leave. Now."

"Or what?" Henry challenged, dismounting with surprising agility for a drunk man. "You'll write about me in your precious newspaper? Ruin what's left of my name?"

"I'll escort you back to town and turn you over to Sheriff Miller," Ezra replied evenly. "This doesn't need to become any more difficult."

Henry gave a harsh laugh. "Always so proper, aren't you, Simmons? So righteous." Without warning, he lunged forward.

Beth cried out as Henry swung wildly at Ezra. Ezra blocked the first blow but wasn't prepared for Henry's sudden ferocity. The second punch caught him squarely in the jaw, sending him staggering backward. Before he could recover, Henry delivered a brutal blow to his temple.

Ezra crumpled to the ground, unconscious.

"Ezra!" Beth rushed toward him, but Henry intercepted her, grabbing her arm with bruising force.

"He'll live," Henry growled, pulling a length of rope from his saddlebag.

Beth struggled against his grip. "Let me go! Help!" she screamed, hoping someone might hear, though she knew they were too far from town.

Henry roughly spun her around, binding her wrists together behind her back with practiced efficiency. Before she could cry out again, he stuffed a handkerchief into her mouth and secured it with another cloth tied around her head.

"You're coming with me," he muttered, dragging her toward his horse. "Might as well get something out of this whole mess."

Beth fought desperately, kicking and twisting, but Henry's strength, fueled by anger and whiskey, overwhelmed her. With a grunt, he hoisted her onto the horse, laying her face-down across the horse like a sack of grain.

She twisted her head, straining for a glimpse of Ezra. He lay motionless on the ground, a trickle of blood running from his temple.

Please, God, let him be alive, she prayed silently, tears stinging her eyes.

Henry mounted behind her, constraining her with one arm while taking the reins with the other. The horse lurched forward, following the creek as it wound behind the edge of town, away from where help might come.

The jolting ride seemed endless. The handkerchief in Beth's mouth tasted of tobacco and whiskey, making her gag. The rope bit into her wrists with each bounce of the horse. Fear and anger warred within her—fear for herself and Ezra, anger at the injustice of this new violation after she'd finally found a place to belong.

Eventually, they approached Henry's house from the rear. It looked even more dilapidated from this angle, with broken window panes and missing shingles. Henry dismounted, dragging Beth roughly from the horse. Her legs, numb from the awkward position, buckled beneath her when he set her down.

"Get up," he ordered, yanking her to her feet by her bound arms.

He kicked in the back door, which hung crookedly on one hinge, and shoved her inside. The kitchen was filthy—unwashed dishes piled in the sink, empty bottles scattered across the table, and a pervasive smell of spoiled food and unwashed bodies. He led her into a bedroom off the kitchen.

"Sit there," Henry commanded, pushing her into a corner. "Don't make a sound."

He removed the gag, but left her hands bound.

"Why are you doing this?" Beth asked, her voice hoarse.

"Because you owe me," Henry snarled, rummaging through a trunk and pulling out a battered carpetbag. "I paid good money for that advertisement. And now you've cost me everything."

"I never intended—"

"I don't care what you intended!" He slammed his fist on the table. "You're mine now. My wife."

Cold dread washed over Beth as she watched him stuff clothes and a bottle of whiskey into the bag.

"We're leaving town," he announced, pausing to take a long drink from the bottle. "Heading west. I've got a cousin in Nevada with a mining claim." His eyes, bloodshot and wild, fixed on her. "You can consider yourself my wife now. For better or worse." He laughed bitterly. "Mostly worse, I expect."

Beth pressed herself more tightly into the corner, mind racing for a way to escape. Ezra might still be unconscious by the creek. No one knew where she was. Henry planned to take her far from Hopewell Creek, from the safety.

From Ezra.

The thought of never seeing him again, of leaving him wounded and worried, pierced her heart more sharply than her fear for herself.

As Henry continued gathering his possessions, muttering angrily to himself, Beth watched the back door, still ajar from their violent entry. Beyond it lay her only hope of freedom, but with her hands bound and Henry just feet away, that hope seemed impossibly distant.

She closed her eyes briefly. Please, Lord, she prayed silently. Help me. Help Ezra. Don't let this be how our story ends.

Henry moved into another room, still cursing and gathering items. Beth stared at the open door, calculating the distance and her chances, wondering desperately what to do.

Chapter 23

Beth stared at the open door, her heart hammering against her ribs. Henry's footsteps creaked in the next room as he continued gathering his belongings. The distance to freedom seemed impossibly vast with her hands bound behind her back, yet she couldn't remain passive. If she stayed, Henry would drag her away from everything she'd come to cherish in Hopewell Creek.

She inched forward, struggling to rise silently from her crouched position without the use of her hands. Her skirt caught beneath her foot, nearly sending her tumbling, but she steadied herself against the wall.

One step. Then another.

The floorboard beneath her right foot groaned. Beth froze, breath catching in her throat.

In the next room, Henry's muttering stopped abruptly.

"Don't you even think about it," he snarled.

Before Beth could make a desperate dash for the door, the front door of the house banged open with such force that the entire structure seemed to shake.

"Beth!" Ezra's voice thundered through the house.

Relief flooded through her so powerfully that her knees nearly buckled. "Here!" she called back. "In the bedroom off the kitchen!"

Heavy boots pounded across the floor. Beth caught a glimpse of Henry's face as he entered the room again—rage giving way to panic as he realized he was cornered.

Ezra burst into the room, a streak of dried blood on his temple, his expression fierce. Sheriff Miller appeared right behind him, revolver drawn and leveled at Henry.

"Don't move, Dobbins," the sheriff commanded, his voice hard as iron. "Not a single inch."

Henry's eyes darted between the door, the sheriff's gun, and the window behind him. His hand twitched toward his belt.

"I wouldn't," Sheriff Miller warned. "You're in enough trouble already. Don't add 'shot while resisting arrest' to your list of misfortunes."

Henry's shoulders slumped, the fight draining from him. "This ain't right," he muttered. "She was supposed to be my wife. She came here for me."

"Under false pretenses," Ezra said, moving carefully to Beth's side while keeping his eyes on Henry. "And abduction is a serious crime, regardless of your twisted justifications."

Sheriff Miller approached Henry cautiously, maintaining his aim. "Turn around, hands behind your back."

When Henry hesitated, the sheriff's voice hardened further. "Now, Dobbins, or I'll consider you a threat."

Henry complied with sullen reluctance. The sheriff efficiently handcuffed him, then patted him down, removing a knife from his belt.

"Beth," Ezra said softly, turning his attention fully to her. His fingers were gentle as he worked at the knots binding her wrists. "Are you hurt?"

She shook her head, unable to speak past the lump in her throat. The relief of seeing him alive and standing before her overwhelmed all other sensations, even the pain, as circulation returned to her hands.

"I was so afraid for you," she whispered when she found her voice. "When he struck you, there was blood, and you weren't moving—"

"I'm alright," he assured her, finally freeing her hands. He took them carefully between his own, rubbing them to help restore circulation. "A hard head runs in the Simmons family, according to my father."

The attempt at humor, despite the gravity of the situation, brought tears to Beth's eyes. She blinked them back, focusing instead on the angry welt forming across Ezra's temple.

"You need a doctor," she said, reaching up to touch the wound before thinking better of it and letting her hand fall.

"So do you," he replied, eyeing the raw marks on her wrists and the bruise forming on her arm where Henry had gripped her.

Sheriff Miller pushed Henry ahead of him toward the door. "I'm taking this reprobate to the jail. Miss Beaumont, Ezra... I'll need a statement from you both, but it can wait until tomorrow."

"Thank you, Sheriff," she said, finding her composure. "How did you know where to find us?"

"Young Jimmy Bellwether," the sheriff explained. "He was fishing downstream and saw the whole thing at the creek. Smart lad ran straight to town and found me, and as he was telling me what he saw, Ezra came stumbling back into town."

"Jimmy said he saw Dobbins knock me unconscious and ride off with you thrown over his horse," Ezra added grimly.

The sheriff nodded. "Wasn't hard to figure where he might take you. His house was the obvious first place to check." He pushed Henry forward. "Come on, Dobbins. You're looking at serious jail time for this."

As they moved through the kitchen toward the front door, Henry twisted his head back, his bloodshot eyes finding Beth's. "This is your fault," he hissed. "All of it. You'll regret this."

"The only one with regrets here is you," Sheriff Miller said, giving him a firm push forward. "And you'll have plenty of time to reflect on them."

When they'd gone, Beth sagged against Ezra, the events of the past hour catching up to her all at once. His arm came around her shoulders, steadying her.

"Let's get you out of here," he said gently.

Beth nodded, but as they started toward the door, she staggered slightly; her legs still weak from being carried across the horse and from the aftermath of fear.

Ezra's arm tightened around her. "Lean on me," he said.

They made their way slowly out of the dilapidated house. The evening air felt gloriously fresh after the stale, whiskey-soured atmosphere inside. Sheriff Miller was already halfway down the street on horseback, marching Henry toward the jail.

A bay gelding was tethered to the porch railing—a sturdy, well-kept animal that Beth recognized as one of the horses the sheriff sometimes rode.

"The sheriff loaned me a horse," Ezra explained.

He helped her sit on the porch steps, then knelt before her, his expression grave as he examined her wrists.

"These need attention," he said, his voice tight. "And your arm where he grabbed you."

"You're the one with a head wound," Beth countered, momentarily distracted from her own discomfort by concern for him.

A ghost of a smile crossed his face. "Then we both need Doc Taylor."

He helped her to her feet and led her to the horse. "Can you ride? It's not far, but—"

"I can manage," she assured him, determined not to appear as shaken as she felt.

Ezra cupped his hands to give her a boost, helping her settle side-saddle onto the horse. Once she was secure, he mounted behind her, one arm coming around her waist to steady her as he took the reins with his other hand.

The proximity was intimate—propriety would normally demand a more formal arrangement—but Beth found herself leaning back against him, drawing comfort from his solid presence and warmth. After the terror of believing she might be dragged away from Hopewell Creek forever, the simple reality of Ezra's heartbeat against her shoulder was profoundly reassuring.

They rode slowly through town, drawing concerned glances from the few people still out as evening approached. Beth kept her gaze forward, too exhausted to manage the social niceties of acknowledging acquaintances.

Chapter 24

Doc Taylor's office was situated in a neat white building with green shutters between the general store and the dressmaker's shop. A small brass plaque beside the door read "Theodore Taylor, M.D." A lamp burned in the window, casting a soft light onto the boardwalk.

Ezra dismounted first, then helped Beth down, his hands gentle on her waist. The world tilted oddly as her feet touched the ground, and she gripped his arms to steady herself.

"Easy," he murmured, concern evident in his eyes. "Doc Taylor will take good care of you."

She nodded, allowing him to guide her to the door. Ezra knocked firmly, and they heard footsteps approaching from within.

The door swung open to reveal a man in his late fifties with graying temples and kind, intelligent eyes behind wire-rimmed spectacles. His expression shifted from polite inquiry to professional concern as he took in their appearance.

"Mr. Simmons, Miss Beaumont," he said, stepping aside to usher them in. "Sheriff Miller sent word you might be coming. Please, come through to the examination room."

The doctor's office was immaculately clean, with the faint scent of carbolic soap and medicinal herbs. He led them to a room containing an examination table, cabinets of supplies, and two straight-backed chairs.

"Miss Beaumont should be examined first," Ezra insisted.

"Nonsense," Beth countered immediately. "Your head wound should take priority."

Doc Taylor smiled slightly. "I believe I'm qualified to determine the order of treatment. Mr. Simmons, please sit. Miss Beaumont, if you'll allow me to examine your wrists and that bruise on your arm..."

He worked efficiently, cleaning the abrasions on Beth's wrists with a mild antiseptic solution that stung but provided almost immediate relief. After examining the bruise on her arm, he applied a soothing salve and wrapped her wrists in clean bandages.

"Nothing broken," he pronounced, "though you'll be sore for several days. Those abrasions should heal cleanly if you keep them clean and dry."

He turned to Ezra next, cleaning the wound on his temple and examining his eyes and responses carefully.

"A mild concussion," the doctor said finally. "You're fortunate it wasn't worse. The scalp tends to bleed dramatically, even with relatively minor injuries."

He applied a small adhesive bandage to the cleaned wound. "I want you to rest tomorrow. No work at the newspaper. Reading and writing will strain your eyes and worsen any headache."

Ezra started to protest, but Doc Taylor cut him off with a raised hand. "Doctor's orders, Mr. Simmons. Miss Beaumont should also rest tomorrow. Her body has undergone significant trauma, even without visible major injuries."

"The Herald—" Ezra began.

"Hopewell Creek will survive without its newspaper for a day," the doctor said firmly. "Your health is more important."

Ezra sighed but nodded, recognizing the wisdom in the doctor's advice. "Thank you, Doc Taylor."

"Think nothing of it." The doctor moved to a cabinet and retrieved two small brown bottles. "Mild pain relief," he explained, handing one to each of them. "Take as needed with water, but no more than three doses in a day."

After ensuring they understood his instructions, Doc Taylor walked them to the door. "I'll look in on both of you tomorrow," he said. "And Miss Beaumont?"

"Yes?"

"I'm deeply sorry for what happened to you today. Please know that Henry Dobbins doesn't represent the character of Hopewell Creek."

The simple kindness in his voice brought unexpected tears to Beth's eyes. "Thank you, Doctor. I've found far more kindness than cruelty here."

Outside, twilight had deepened toward night. Ezra helped Beth onto the sheriff's horse again, mounting behind her as before. This time, she didn't hesitate to lean against him, too weary to pretend a strength she didn't feel.

They rode toward Mrs. Jenkins' boarding house at a gentle pace. The town had grown quiet. Most residents were already at home for their evening meals. A few lamps glowed in windows, creating pools of light that seemed to emphasize the gathering darkness between them.

As they approached the boarding house, Beth saw a figure on the front porch—Mrs. Jenkins, pacing anxiously in the glow of the porch lamp. When she spotted them, she hurried down the steps to meet them.

"Thank the Lord," she exclaimed, her normally composed face creased with worry. "I've been beside myself since I heard."

Ezra dismounted and helped Beth down. Mrs. Jenkins immediately moved to Beth's side, supporting her with a motherly arm around her shoulders.

"Tom Bellwether told me what happened when he came by to drop off some repaired kitchen items," Mrs. Jenkins explained. "He said Jimmy saw the whole thing at the creek. The poor boy was quite shaken."

She urged them toward the house. "Come inside, both of you. You need hot coffee and a proper meal."

"Mrs. Jenkins, I would rather not impose," Ezra began, but she cut him off with a wave of her hand.

"Nonsense. After what you've both been through, the very least I can do is feed you properly. Besides," she added, with a pointed look at his bandaged temple, "you shouldn't be alone tonight with a head injury."

Mrs. Jenkins guided them to the parlor. "Sit down before you fall down," she instructed. "I'll bring coffee and supper on trays. You both look done in."

Left alone in the parlor, Beth and Ezra settled onto the sofa. The events of the day seemed surreal now, in the civilized comfort of Mrs. Jenkins' parlor.

"Are you truly alright?" Ezra asked quietly, his eyes searching her face.

"I will be," Beth answered honestly. "It was terrifying, but..." She hesitated, finding the courage to speak from her heart. "Knowing you came for me made all the difference."

A shadow crossed his face. "I should never have let it happen in the first place. When he struck me, and I couldn't protect you—"

"No," Beth interrupted firmly. "You mustn't blame yourself. Henry Dobbins is responsible for his own actions, not you."

Ezra's expression softened. "You're remarkable, Beth Beaumont."

The way he looked at her—as though she were precious beyond measure—made her breath catch.

"At the creek," she said, her voice barely above a whisper, "before Henry interrupted... you were about to tell me something."

Ezra nodded slowly, his eyes never leaving hers. "I was." He took a deep breath, as though gathering courage. "Beth, when you came to Hopewell Creek, I thought I was merely gaining an assistant for the Herald. I never expected..."

He paused, searching for words. "I never expected to find someone who would change how I see everything. Who would make each day brighter simply by being part of it."

Beth's heart thundered in her chest as he continued.

"I know it hasn't been long, but sometimes God's greatest blessings arrive unexpectedly." He turned toward her and reached for her hand, careful of her bandaged wrist, and held it gently between both of his. "I've fallen in love with you, Beth. Deeply, completely in love. If you'll have me, I want to court you properly, with the intention of building a life together."

The words she'd secretly longed to hear, yet hardly dared to believe possible, hung in the air between them. Beth felt tears gather in her eyes—not of sorrow or fear this time, but of a joy so profound it ached.

"Ezra," she said, her voice unsteady. "When I came to Hopewell Creek, I was running from pain and disappointment. I never dreamed I might find such happiness here." She drew a steadying breath. "I've fallen in love with you, too."

The smile that transformed his face was like a sunrise after the longest night. With exquisite gentleness, he raised one hand to her cheek, his thumb brushing away a tear that had escaped.

"May I kiss you, Beth?" he asked softly.

She nodded, unable to find words past the swell of emotion in her throat.

Ezra leaned toward her slowly, giving her time to withdraw if she wished. His lips touched hers with such tenderness that fresh tears sprang to her eyes. The kiss was gentle, reverent—a promise rather than a demand.

When he drew back, Beth felt transformed, as though the world had shifted on its axis, rearranging itself around this new, precious reality they had created together.

"I love you," Ezra said simply, his voice rough with emotion.

"And I love you," Beth replied, the words feeling like coming home after a long journey.

The sound of footsteps in the hallway reminded them of where they were. They moved slightly apart, though Ezra kept hold of her hand as Mrs. Jenkins entered the parlor carrying a large tray.

If she noticed their clasped hands or the heightened color in their cheeks, she gave no sign of it, merely setting the tray on the low table before them.

"Coffee, chicken noodle soup, and fresh bread," she announced.

"This is very kind of you, Mrs. Jenkins," Beth said, suddenly realizing how hungry she was.

"It's the least I can do," Mrs. Jenkins replied, pouring coffee for them both. "Now eat while it's hot. You both need your strength."

She bustled out again, leaving them to their meal.

"Ezra," Beth said eventually, setting down her spoon. "Your head—you must be in pain. Shouldn't you take some of the medicine Doc Taylor provided?"

"Later, perhaps," he said, though she noticed he'd been squinting slightly. "It's not so bad."

"You're a terrible liar," she said with gentle affection. "Please take it. For my peace of mind, if nothing else."

He smiled ruefully. "Very well. For your peace of mind."

Mrs. Jenkins returned with water and watched approvingly as Ezra took a dose of the pain medication. After clearing their empty dishes, she brought an apple cobbler topped with fresh cream.

"Mrs. Jenkins," Ezra said as she served the dessert, "I want to thank you for taking such good care of Beth since her arrival in Hopewell Creek. Your kindness has meant more than you know."

The older woman's expression softened. "She's been a joy to have here." She glanced at Beth with genuine affection.

As they finished their dessert, Mrs. Jenkins stood with an air of making a decision. "Now, Miss Beaumont needs her rest after such an ordeal. And you, Mr. Simmons, certainly shouldn't be riding home in the dark with a head injury."

"I wouldn't want to impose—" Ezra began.

"It's no imposition," Mrs. Jenkins said firmly. "I keep a spare room ready for emergencies, and I'd consider this an emergency. You'll stay here tonight, where I can keep an eye on you both."

Her tone brooked no argument. Ezra looked at Beth, who gave a small nod of agreement.

"Thank you, Mrs. Jenkins," he said. "That's very kind."

"It's simple common sense," she replied, but looked pleased nonetheless. "I'll go prepare the room."

When she had gone, Ezra turned to Beth. "She reminds me of my mother—impossible to argue with when she's made up her mind."

Beth smiled. "I'm glad she insisted. I'd worry about you riding home alone."

"Would you?" There was a warmth in his eyes that made her blush.

"Of course." She hesitated, then added, "I care about you a great deal, Ezra."

"And I care about you." His expression grew serious. "Beth, I meant what I said earlier. I want to court you properly, with respect and honor. My intentions are—"

"I know," she interrupted gently. "I trust you, Ezra. Completely."

The simple statement seemed to move him deeply. He raised her hand to his lips, pressing a kiss to her knuckles.

"I'll strive to be worthy of that trust," he promised.

Mrs. Jenkins returned then, effectively ending their private conversation. "The room is ready, Mr. Simmons. And Miss Beaumont, you should retire as well. It's been a most trying day."

They stood, suddenly awkward in the transition from intimate conversation to social propriety.

"I'll see you in the morning," Ezra said, his eyes conveying far more than his words.

"Yes," Beth replied, finding herself smiling despite her weariness. "In the morning."

Mrs. Jenkins led Ezra upstairs to the spare room, while Beth followed more slowly, each step reminding her of the day's physical exertions.

In the sanctuary of her own room, Beth closed the door and leaned against it, overwhelmed by the tumult of emotions the day had brought. Terror and despair had given way to relief, and then to a joy so profound it seemed almost unreal.

She moved to her washstand and carefully cleaned her face, mindful of her bandaged wrists. After changing into her nightgown, she sat at the small vanity to brush her hair, her movements automatic as her mind revisited Ezra's declaration.

He loves me, she thought, the reality of it still astonishing. The man she'd come to admire so deeply—his intelligence, his integrity, his kindness—returned her feelings.

Her fingers rose unconsciously to touch her lips, remembering the gentle pressure of his kiss—her very first kiss. She hadn't realized until this moment that she'd never been kissed by a man before. The realization made the memory all the more precious.

Beth set down her hairbrush and moved to the window, looking out at the quiet street below. Somehow, against all odds, she had found her place in this town. More than that, she had found love—a possibility that would have seemed ludicrous just weeks ago when she'd fled St. Louis in desperation.

Drawing the curtains, Beth turned to her bed. Before climbing beneath the covers, she knelt beside it, folding her hands in prayer.

"Dear Lord," she whispered, "thank You for Your protection today. Thank You for guiding Jimmy to witness what happened, for bringing help to me through Ezra and the sheriff."

She paused, emotion welling up in her throat.

"Thank You for leading me to Hopewell Creek, even through such an unlikely path. Thank You for Mrs. Jenkins' kindness, for Maggie's friendship, for the welcome I've found in this community."

Tears slipped down her cheeks as she continued.

"Most of all, thank You for Ezra. For his goodness, his strength, his faith. For the love we've found together." Her voice broke slightly. "I don't know what plans You have for us, Lord, but I'm grateful beyond words for this blessing."

***

Across the hallway, Ezra sat on the edge of the spare room bed, his head aching despite the medicine but his heart fuller than he could remember it being in years.

"Thank You, Lord," he whispered into the quiet room. "For bringing her safely back. For the gift of her love. Whatever lies ahead, I'll cherish and protect her as long as You grant me the privilege of walking by her side."

He stretched out on the bed, not bothering to remove more than his boots and jacket, too weary to manage anything else. As sleep claimed him, his last conscious thought was of Beth's smile when he'd told her he loved her—a smile that had illuminated something that had long been missing in his life and now felt wonderfully, miraculously complete.

Chapter 25

Morning light filtered through the curtains when Beth awoke. For a moment, she lay still, taking inventory of her body's complaints—sore wrists, stiff muscles, a tender spot on her back where she'd bounced against the saddle. But she was safe in her own bed, and that knowledge overshadowed all discomfort.

A soft knock at her door roused her fully. "Beth? Are you awake, dear?" Mrs. Jenkins called.

"Yes, come in," Beth replied, sitting up against her pillows.

Mrs. Jenkins entered, carrying a breakfast tray. "I thought you might appreciate breakfast in bed this morning," she said kindly. "How are you feeling?"

"Much better after a night's rest," Beth assured her, though this wasn't entirely true—her body felt as though she'd been dragged behind a horse rather than carried across one. "Is Ezra still here?"

"He left about an hour ago," Mrs. Jenkins replied, setting the tray across Beth's lap. "Insisted on going to the Herald, despite what the doctor said. That young man is stubborn as a mule sometimes."

Beth smiled, imagining Ezra's determination to maintain his routine despite his injury. "That doesn't surprise me."

"He did leave this for you." Mrs. Jenkins handed her a folded note. "Now eat your breakfast while it's hot. I'll come back for the tray later."

After Mrs. Jenkins departed, Beth unfolded the note with eager fingers.

Beth,

I hope you slept well and are feeling stronger this morning. I've gone to the Herald to take care of some essential matters, though I promise to heed Dr. Taylor's advice about rest.

Please don't concern yourself with work today. The newspaper will survive without you for one day.

With deepest affection,

Ezra

P.S. I meant every word I said last night, and I look forward to continuing our conversation when you feel ready.

Heat rose to Beth's cheeks at the postscript, and she found herself touching her lips with her fingertips, remembering the gentle pressure of his kiss. She read the note twice more before setting it aside to eat her breakfast—eggs, toast, and hot tea, all perfectly prepared.

As she ate, Beth contemplated the dramatic shift in her circumstances. Just weeks ago, she had been desperate enough to flee St. Louis as a mail-order bride, with no certainty of what awaited her. Now, despite yesterday's trauma—or perhaps partially because of it—she felt more secure than she had in years.

She had meaningful work that utilized her intelligence. She had friends who cared for her welfare. And she had Ezra, whose feelings for her seemed to match the growing depth of her own.

After finishing her breakfast, Beth washed and dressed carefully, choosing her blue calico dress—the one Ezra had complimented. She was brushing her hair when another knock came at her door.

"Beth?" Mrs. Jenkins called. "Sheriff Miller is here to see you."

"I'll be right down," Beth responded, quickly pinning her hair into a neat arrangement.

The sheriff waited in the parlor, hat in hand, his expression softening when Beth entered.

"Miss Beaumont," he greeted her, "I hope you're recovering from yesterday's ordeal."

"I am, thank you," Beth replied, taking a seat across from him. "How may I help you, Sheriff?"

"I need your account of what happened," he explained, pulling out a small notebook and pencil. "For my official report and potential testimony, should Dobbins' case go to trial."

For the next half-hour, Beth recounted the events at the creek and Henry's cabin as accurately as she could remember them. Sheriff Miller took careful notes, occasionally asking for clarification, but never interrupting her narrative.

"You've been very brave, Miss Beaumont," he said when she finished. "Not many would maintain such composure after what you experienced."

"I had faith help would come," Beth replied honestly. "Though I was prepared to attempt escape if necessary."

The sheriff nodded approvingly. "That's good thinking." He closed his notebook and tucked it into his pocket. "Dobbins will be transferred to the county jail tomorrow. There's enough evidence to hold him for fraud, kidnapping, and assault. He won't trouble Hopewell Creek again."

"What will happen to him?" Beth asked.

"He'll likely serve several years in territorial prison," Sheriff Miller answered. "Particularly, once we investigate his previous mail-order bride schemes. There's some concern about those other women who came to town and then disappeared."

A chill ran through Beth at the implication. "Do you think he...?"

The sheriff's expression turned grim. "I can't say for certain. But I intend to find out."

After the sheriff departed, promising to keep her informed of developments, Beth found herself at loose ends. The thought of spending the entire day alone with her thoughts was unappealing.

"Mrs. Jenkins," she called, finding her landlady in the kitchen, "would it be all right if I walked into town? I feel the need for fresh air and activity."

Mrs. Jenkins looked concerned. "Are you certain you're up to it? You've been through quite an ordeal."

"I am," Beth assured her. "Staying idle will only give me too much time to dwell on yesterday's events. Besides, I thought I might visit Maggie at the café. We missed our supper engagement last night."

"Well, in that case," Mrs. Jenkins conceded, "a short walk might do you good. But promise you'll return if you tire."

"I promise," Beth agreed readily.

The walk into town proved exactly what Beth needed. The spring air was fresh and invigorating, birds sang in the trees lining the main street, and the familiar sights of Hopewell Creek's bustling businesses reassured her that life continued normally despite her personal drama.

Several townspeople greeted her warmly, though a few cast curious glances at her bandaged wrists. News traveled quickly in Hopewell

Creek, and Beth suspected most knew at least the outline of what had happened with Henry Dobbins.

As she passed the Herald office, Beth hesitated, tempted to stop in and see Ezra. But his note had been clear—she should rest today—and she wouldn't undermine his concern by appearing at work. Instead, she continued to the O'Leary Café, where Maggie spotted her immediately from behind the counter.

"Beth!" Maggie exclaimed, rushing around to embrace her gently. "Oh, I've been so worried! We missed you at supper last night, and then we heard what that horrible man did."

Beth returned the hug, touched by Maggie's genuine concern. "I'm fine, truly. Just a bit sore and shaken."

Maggie led her to a table in the corner, away from the few other mid-morning customers. "Mother!" she called toward the kitchen. "Beth's here!"

Mrs. O'Leary emerged, wiping her hands on her apron. Her normally cheerful face was creased with concern as she approached Beth's table.

"My dear girl," she said, patting Beth's shoulder. "What a terrible experience you've had. Are you truly all right?"

"Yes, thanks to Ezra and Sheriff Miller," Beth assured her. "And I'm sorry about missing our supper plans."

"Nonsense." Mrs. O'Leary dismissed the apology with a wave. "The important thing is that you're safe. Now, you'll have tea and fresh scones, and I won't hear a word against it."

Before Beth could respond, Mrs. O'Leary had bustled back to the kitchen, leaving her and Maggie alone.

"Mother's solution to all of life's troubles is food," Maggie explained with an affectionate smile. "And I must say, it's usually effective."

Beth laughed softly. "I'm finding that to be true."

Maggie leaned forward, her expression turning serious. "Is it true that Ezra rescued you from Henry Dobbins' cabin? Everyone's talking about it, but you know how stories grow with each telling."

Beth nodded, recounting a simplified version of the previous day's events.

"How romantic," Maggie sighed when Beth finished. "Terrible and frightening, of course," she added hastily, "but also quite heroic of Ezra."

"It was," Beth agreed, feeling her cheeks warm slightly.

Maggie's eyes narrowed shrewdly. "There's something you're not telling me. I can see it in your face."

Before Beth could respond, Mrs. O'Leary returned with a tray bearing tea and warm scones with clotted cream and jam. Beth used the interruption to gather her thoughts, uncertain how much she wanted to share about her changed relationship with Ezra.

Once Mrs. O'Leary had gone, however, Maggie fixed Beth with an expectant look. "Well? What aren't you sharing?"

Beth took a sip of tea, then set the cup down carefully. "Ezra and I... that is, before Henry appeared, we were having a rather significant conversation."

"What kind of significant?" Maggie prompted, her eyes bright with interest.

"He told me his feelings for me had grown beyond friendship," Beth admitted, unable to suppress a small smile. "And I confessed the same."

Maggie clapped her hands softly. "I knew it! Anyone with eyes could see how he looks at you."

"And later, at Mrs. Jenkins' house..." Beth hesitated, then continued quietly, "he kissed me."

"Beth Beaumont!" Maggie exclaimed, then lowered her voice when several patrons turned to look. "Your first kiss?"

Beth nodded, flushing deeply.

"Was it wonderful?" Maggie asked eagerly. "I've always thought Ezra would be a considerate kisser."

"Maggie!" Beth protested, scandalized and amused in equal measure. "I can't believe you've thought about that."

"Oh, every unmarried woman in Hopewell Creek has considered Ezra Simmons as a potential husband at some point," Maggie replied matter-of-factly. "He's handsome, intelligent, and kind. But he's never shown a particular interest in anyone." Her smile turned impish. "Until you."

Beth shook her head, bemused by Maggie's forthrightness. "To answer your question, yes, it was... quite wonderful. Very gentle."

"I knew it," Maggie declared triumphantly. "So what happens now?"

"I'm not entirely sure," Beth admitted. "Everything has happened so quickly. Just a few weeks ago, I was in St. Louis, desperate enough to answer a mail-order bride advertisement. Now I'm here, with work I enjoy and..." she hesitated, "feelings for someone I respect tremendously."

"Life changes quickly sometimes," Maggie observed. "My mother always said when God decides to move into your life, He doesn't always send a written itinerary first."

Beth laughed. "Your mother is so wise."

"She is," Maggie confirmed with a fond smile. "Irish to her bones and full of sayings for every occasion." She reached across the table to squeeze Beth's hand gently. "I'm glad you're in Hopewell Creek, Beth. Not just for Ezra's sake, but because you've become a dear friend in such a short time."

Beth felt her throat tighten with emotion. "Thank you, Maggie. That means more than I can express."

They finished their tea and scones; the conversation turning to lighter topics—the upcoming box social at church, the town dance, Maggie's new dress pattern, and the early summer flowers beginning to bloom in the churchyard.

As Beth prepared to leave, promising to return for supper that evening if she felt well enough, the café door opened. Rosalind Fairfield entered, elegantly dressed as always, in a fashionable walking suit of deep green.

Her eyes widened slightly at the sight of Beth, then narrowed calculatingly. "Miss Beaumont," she greeted with artificial sweetness. "I'd heard you had quite an adventure yesterday. How fortunate that Ezra came to your rescue."

The words were polite, but her tone carried a distinct edge of mockery.

"Yes, I was very fortunate," Beth agreed evenly, determined not to let Rosalind provoke her.

"Ezra has always had a knight-errant streak," Rosalind continued, removing her gloves deliberately. "Such a tender heart for those in... unfortunate circumstances."

The implication that Beth was merely an object of pity stung, but Beth maintained her composure. "Mr. Simmons is indeed a man of admirable character."

Rosalind's smile tightened. "Yes, well. One hopes his charitable impulses don't lead him into unwise entanglements."

Maggie stepped forward, her normally cheerful face unusually stern. "Is there something I can help you with today, Miss Fairfield? Mother's baked fresh apple turnovers."

Rosalind's attention shifted reluctantly. "Just tea, thank you. I'm meeting Father here to discuss the Literary Society's summer reading selections."

"I'll prepare it right away," Maggie replied, her tone making it clear the conversation was over.

"If you'll excuse me," Beth said politely, "I should be returning to Mrs. Jenkins."

"Of course," Rosalind replied, her gaze uncomfortably assessing. "Do take care, Miss Beaumont."

Chapter 26

Outside, Beth took a deep breath of fresh air, trying to shake off the unpleasant encounter with Rosalind.

As she approached the newspaper office, the door opened, and Ezra emerged, looking tired but alert. His face brightened visibly when he spotted her.

"Beth," he called, crossing the street to meet her. "I didn't expect to see you in town today."

"I needed fresh air and company," she explained. "I've been visiting with Maggie."

Ezra studied her face carefully. "How are you feeling?"

"Better," she assured him. "Sheriff Miller took my statement this morning."

Ezra nodded. "He spoke with me as well. Dobbins will face serious charges."

They stood in silence for a moment, both aware of the shift in their relationship, but uncertain how to navigate it in broad daylight on the main street.

"I was just closing the office," Ezra finally said. "Would you care to join me at the café for a cup of coffee?"

Beth hesitated, thinking of Rosalind waiting there. "Actually, I've just come from there. Perhaps we could walk by the creek instead? If you're not too busy."

Something in her tone or expression must have alerted him. "Has something happened?"

"Not exactly," Beth hedged. "I encountered Rosalind at the café. She was... less than kind."

Ezra's expression darkened. "What did she say?"

"Nothing overtly offensive," Beth assured him. "Just implications that your interest in me stems from pity rather than genuine regard."

"That's absurd," Ezra stated firmly. "And typical of Rosalind when she feels threatened."

"Threatened?" Beth repeated, surprised.

Ezra's smile was both rueful and tender. "She's observed what I myself was slow to recognize—that my feelings for you are unlike anything I've experienced before."

Despite the public setting, Beth felt her heart flutter at his words. "Ezra..."

"The creek sounds perfect," he said, offering his arm. "Shall we?"

Beth placed her hand in the crook of his elbow, aware of curious glances from passersby, but finding she didn't mind. They walked in comfortable silence until they reached the outskirts of town.

"I must admit," Ezra said as they followed the path through the cottonwoods, "I was concerned about returning here after yesterday's events."

"As was I," Beth confessed. "But I refuse to let Henry Dobbins taint this place. It was peaceful and beautiful before he intruded, and it can be so again."

Ezra nodded approvingly. "You're remarkably resilient, Beth Beaumont."

They reached the creek bank, stopping at a different spot from the day before. The water flowed clear and swift, sunlight dancing on its surface. Birds called in the trees overhead, and a gentle breeze stirred the new leaves.

"I've been thinking," Ezra said after they'd stood quietly for a moment, "about what happens next."

Beth turned to face him, heart quickening. "And?"

His eyes, earnest and warm, met hers. "I meant what I said yesterday, and what I wrote in my note. My feelings for you have grown into something profound and lasting."

"As have mine for you," Beth replied softly.

"I do want to court you properly," Ezra stated, taking both her hands gently in his. "With clear intentions and the respect you deserve."

Joy bloomed in Beth's heart, bright and unexpected. "I would like that very much."

"I know it's been less than a month since you arrived in Hopewell Creek," Ezra continued, his thumbs tracing gentle circles on the backs of her hands. "And some might consider this hasty. But I believe some things in life don't require prolonged deliberation when they're clearly right."

"I agree," Beth said, squeezing his hands lightly. "What I feel for you isn't hasty or ill-considered, despite the short time we've known each other. It's..." she searched for the right words, "it's as though I recognized something in you that I've always known was possible but never found."

Ezra's smile was radiant. "Exactly so. Like coming home to a place you've never been before, but somehow always belonged."

"Yes," Beth breathed, marveling at how perfectly he'd captured her feelings.

Still holding her hands, Ezra bent his head slowly toward hers, his eyes silently seeking permission. Beth tilted her face up to meet him, and their lips joined in a kiss more assured than the first but equally tender.

When they separated, Ezra rested his forehead against hers for a moment. "I've been wanting to do that again since last night," he admitted.

Beth smiled. "As have I."

They walked along the creek for a while longer, talking easily about their hopes for the future. Ezra spoke of improvements he wanted to make to the Herald, perhaps expanding to a twice-weekly publication as the town grew. Beth shared her thoughts about possibly teaching someday, particularly if the school expanded as planned.

"Whatever paths we choose," Ezra said as they turned back toward town, "I hope we'll walk them together."

The simple statement, spoken without excessive sentiment but with absolute sincerity, touched Beth deeply. "I hope so too."

As they approached the edge of town and the church came into view, Beth turned to Ezra and said, "Let's go inside for a moment, shall we?"

Ezra's expression softened. "I'd like that very much."

The small white church stood serene against the afternoon sky, its steeple reaching toward heaven like a finger pointing the way. When they climbed the steps, Ezra pushed open the heavy wooden door, which swung inward with a familiar creak.

Inside, the church was empty and peaceful. Sunlight streamed through the stained-glass windows, casting jewel-toned patterns across the worn wooden pews. Their footsteps echoed softly as they walked down the center aisle, still hand in hand.

At the front of the church, they knelt together before the simple altar. The scent of beeswax candles and old hymnals surrounded them, comforting in its familiarity.

Ezra bowed his head, still holding Beth's hand gently in his own, mindful of her bandaged wrists. After a moment of silence, he began to pray, his deep voice resonating in the quiet sanctuary.

"Heavenly Father," he began, "we come before You today with grateful hearts. When we look back on the path that brought us here—the trials, the choices, the seeming coincidences—we see Your hand guiding us every step of the way."

Beth felt tears welling behind her closed eyelids as Ezra continued.

"Thank You for bringing Beth safely to Hopewell Creek, Lord, even through such unexpected and difficult circumstances. Thank You for protecting her from harm and giving us both the courage to face danger yesterday. Your mercy has been abundant beyond measure."

His voice grew softer, more intimate. "Father, we thank You for this gift we've found in each other—this connection that neither of us was seeking, but that You, in Your perfect wisdom, orchestrated. We recognize it as a blessing from Your hand."

Beth felt a tear slip down her cheek as Ezra's thumb gently traced over her knuckles.

"Guide us, Lord, as we walk forward together. Help us to build something that honors You in all ways. Give us wisdom to know Your will, patience to wait for Your timing, and courage to follow where You lead. Teach us to love each other as You have loved us—selflessly, faithfully, and completely."

His voice caught slightly on the words, and Beth opened her eyes to see a matching tear tracking down Ezra's cheek, illuminated by a shaft of colored light from the stained-glass window.

"We surrender our future to You, knowing that Your plans for us are greater than anything we could imagine for ourselves. May our relationship glorify You and be a testimony to Your goodness and faithfulness."

He paused, then added softly, "Thank You, Father, for second chances and new beginnings. For bringing light from darkness and joy from sorrow. For making all things new."

"Amen," Beth whispered, her heart too full for more words.

"Amen," Ezra echoed, opening his eyes to meet hers.

For a long moment, they remained kneeling together in the sunlit church, their joined hands a promise, their shared prayer a covenant. In this sacred space, Beth felt the final pieces of her heart healing—not just her feelings for Ezra, but her faith in God's goodness, which had been tested but never truly lost.

Outside, the town of Hopewell Creek continued its daily rhythms. The creek flowed ever onward; the cottonwoods rustled in the spring breeze, and life moved forward as it always had. But for Beth and Ezra, everything had changed. What had begun as a desperate escape and a practical arrangement had transformed into something beautiful and lasting—a love story written not by chance, but by divine design.

As they finally rose and walked back down the aisle together, Beth knew with absolute certainty that she had found what she had always sought—not just a place to belong, but a person to belong with, and a faith strong enough to sustain them both through whatever lay ahead.

In the dappled light of the church, with Ezra's hand warm and steady in hers, Beth Beaumont was finally, truly home.

Leave A Review

I f you enjoyed this book, please consider leaving an honest review on Amazon

Visit Our Website:

www.vivianbelle.com

Visit Our Amazon Author Page

Find Us On Social Media:

Facebook

Facebook Author Page

Instagram